TWISTED JOURNEYS #20

PERIL AT SUMMERLAND PARK

PAUL D. STORRIE

ILLUSTRATED BY SANDY CARRUTHERS

GRAPHIC UNIVERSE™ · M

Story by Paul D. Storrie

Pencils and inks by Sandy Carruthers

Coloring by Studio C10

Lettering by Marshall Dillon

Copyright © 2012 by Lerner Publishing Group, Inc.

Graphic Universe™ is a trademark and Twisted Journeys® is a registered trademark of Lerner Publishing Group, Inc.

Graphic Universe
A division of Lerner Publishing Group, Inc.
241 First Avenue North
Minneapolis, MN 55401 U.S.A.

Website address: www.lernerbooks.com

Main body text set in Myriad Tilt Bold 14/16. Typeface provided by Adobe Systems.

Library of Congress Cataloging-in-Publication Data

Storrie, Paul D.
     Peril at Summerland Park / by Paul D. Storrie ; illustrated by Sandy Carruthers.
       p. cm. — (Twisted journeys ; #20)
     Summary: The reader's choices guide three teenagers as they explore the ruins of an amusement park with a shady history.
     ISBN: 978-0-7613-4935-8 (lib. bdg. : alk. paper)
     1. Plot-your-own stories. 2. Graphic novels. [1. Graphic novels. 2. Amusement parks—Fiction. 3. Plot-your-own stories.] I. Carruthers, Sandy, ill. II. Title.
PZ7.7.S756Pe 2012
741.5'973—dc22   2011009941

Manufactured in the United States of America
1 – BC – 12/31/11

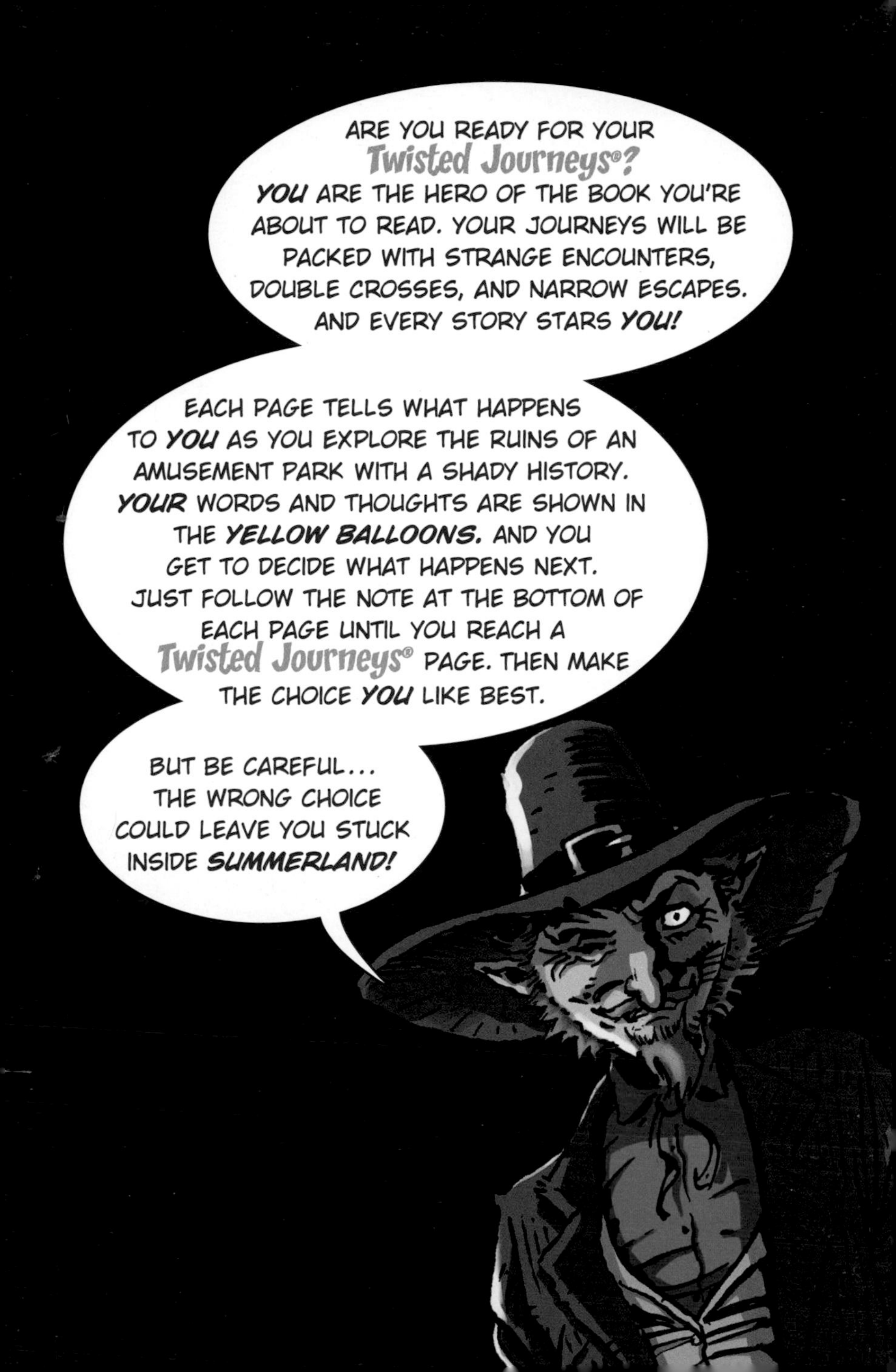
ARE YOU READY FOR YOUR Twisted Journeys®? YOU ARE THE HERO OF THE BOOK YOU'RE ABOUT TO READ. YOUR JOURNEYS WILL BE PACKED WITH STRANGE ENCOUNTERS, DOUBLE CROSSES, AND NARROW ESCAPES. AND EVERY STORY STARS YOU!
EACH PAGE TELLS WHAT HAPPENS TO YOU AS YOU EXPLORE THE RUINS OF AN AMUSEMENT PARK WITH A SHADY HISTORY. YOUR WORDS AND THOUGHTS ARE SHOWN IN THE YELLOW BALLOONS. AND YOU GET TO DECIDE WHAT HAPPENS NEXT. JUST FOLLOW THE NOTE AT THE BOTTOM OF EACH PAGE UNTIL YOU REACH A Twisted Journeys® PAGE. THEN MAKE THE CHOICE YOU LIKE BEST.
BUT BE CAREFUL... THE WRONG CHOICE COULD LEAVE YOU STUCK INSIDE SUMMERLAND!

You've arrived!

You and your friends, Rick and Laura, traveled all day to reach Summerland Amusement Park in Michigan's Irish Hills. Rick and Laura share an interest in the paranormal—unexplained events and legendary creatures—and it's hard for you not to be a little curious.

Summerland has been closed for nearly twenty years, but *why* it closed is what brought you here. When it was open, the park got a reputation for being an incredibly unlucky place. At first it was little things—a few too many people losing hats or purses. Later, there were problems with the rides and strange, even deadly accidents. Eventually, the park had to close. Not long ago, you heard the story of Summerland and decided to check it out. Maybe even find proof that it's haunted or cursed! But first you have to get inside.

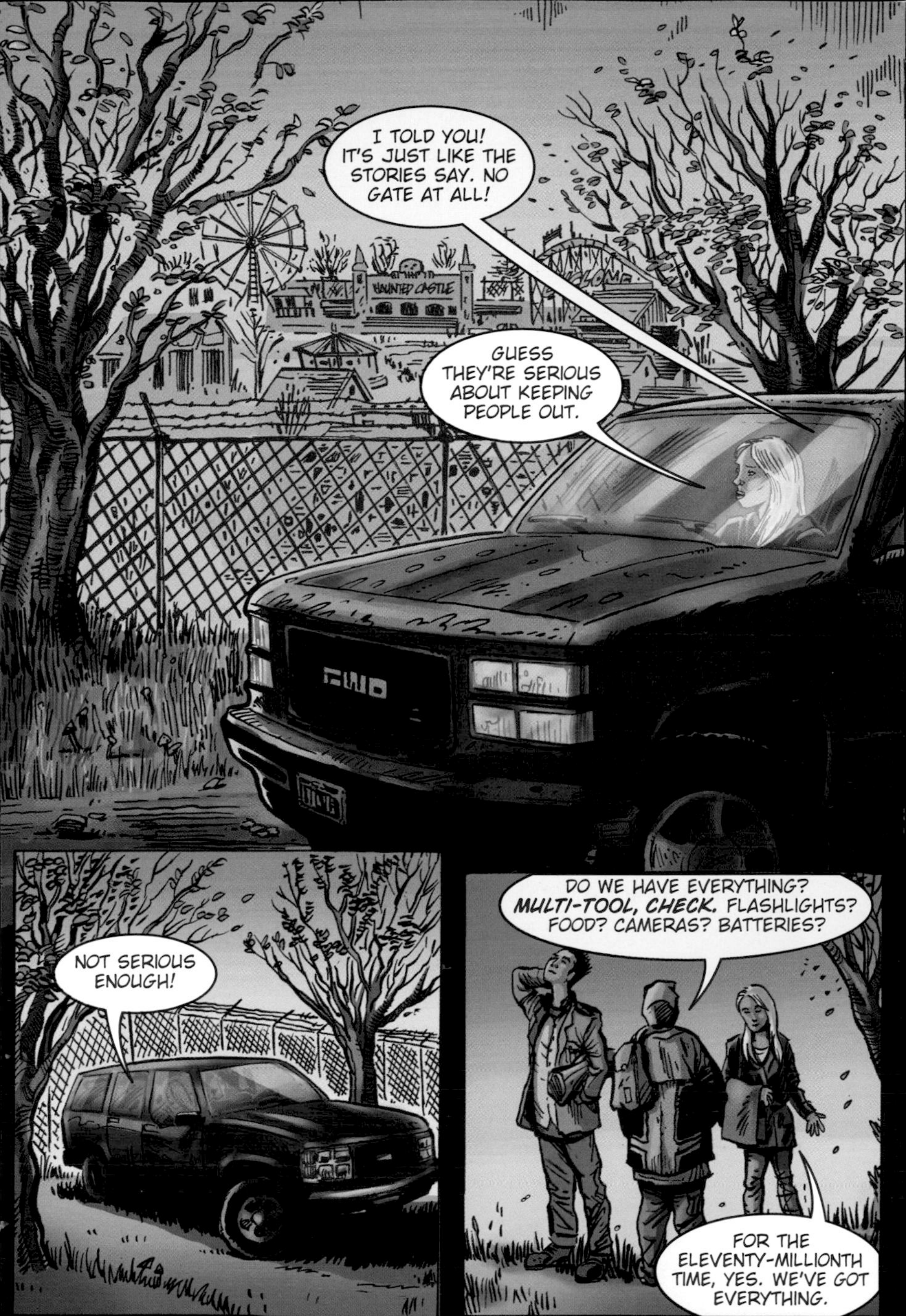
HAUNTED CASTLE
I TOLD YOU! IT'S JUST LIKE THE STORIES SAY. NO GATE AT ALL!
GUESS THEY'RE SERIOUS ABOUT KEEPING PEOPLE OUT.
NOT SERIOUS ENOUGH!
DO WE HAVE EVERYTHING? MULTI-TOOL, CHECK. FLASHLIGHTS? FOOD? CAMERAS? BATTERIES?
FOR THE ELEVENTY-MILLIONTH TIME, YES. WE'VE GOT EVERYTHING.

GO ON TO THE NEXT PAGE.

With a grin, you climb up the hood of the SUV onto the roof. You take a running start and leap over the fence. On the other side, you hit the ground and roll. Getting up, you wave for your friends to follow.

Laura tosses you the blanket and jumps. Rick is right behind her. You drop the blanket near the fence so you'll have it to cover the barbed wire when you climb back out.

Laura nods and says, "Let's do this!"

Soon you're on the midway.

Rick lets out a whistle. "This is awesome!"

"So," you say, "where should we start?"

A gravelly voice startles you from behind: "Maybe ye should start by explaining how ye got in where you're not meant to be?"

The three of you spin around to see a strange old man dressed all in red.

You didn't expect anyone to be
inside Summerland!

WILL YOU . . .

. . . try to make a getaway?
TURN TO PAGE 16.

. . . try to explain why you're where
you shouldn't be?
TURN TO PAGE 46.

Laura gulps. "This is bad." The spriggans start toward you.

"It's okay," Rick says. "We've got iron. Let's get 'em."

You flip open your multi-tool. "There's also the element of surprise."

The spriggans hesitate when they see the multi-tool in your hand. One of them squints, giving it a good look. "Iron?" he mutters.

You hold it out toward them, trying to look scary. "That's right! You don't want to mess with iron!"

Rick shakes his flashlight at them. "Yeah! Back off! Don't make me thump your ugly skulls."

Laura looks worried. "Maybe fewer threats and more bargaining?" she whispers.

8

GO ON TO THE NEXT PAGE.

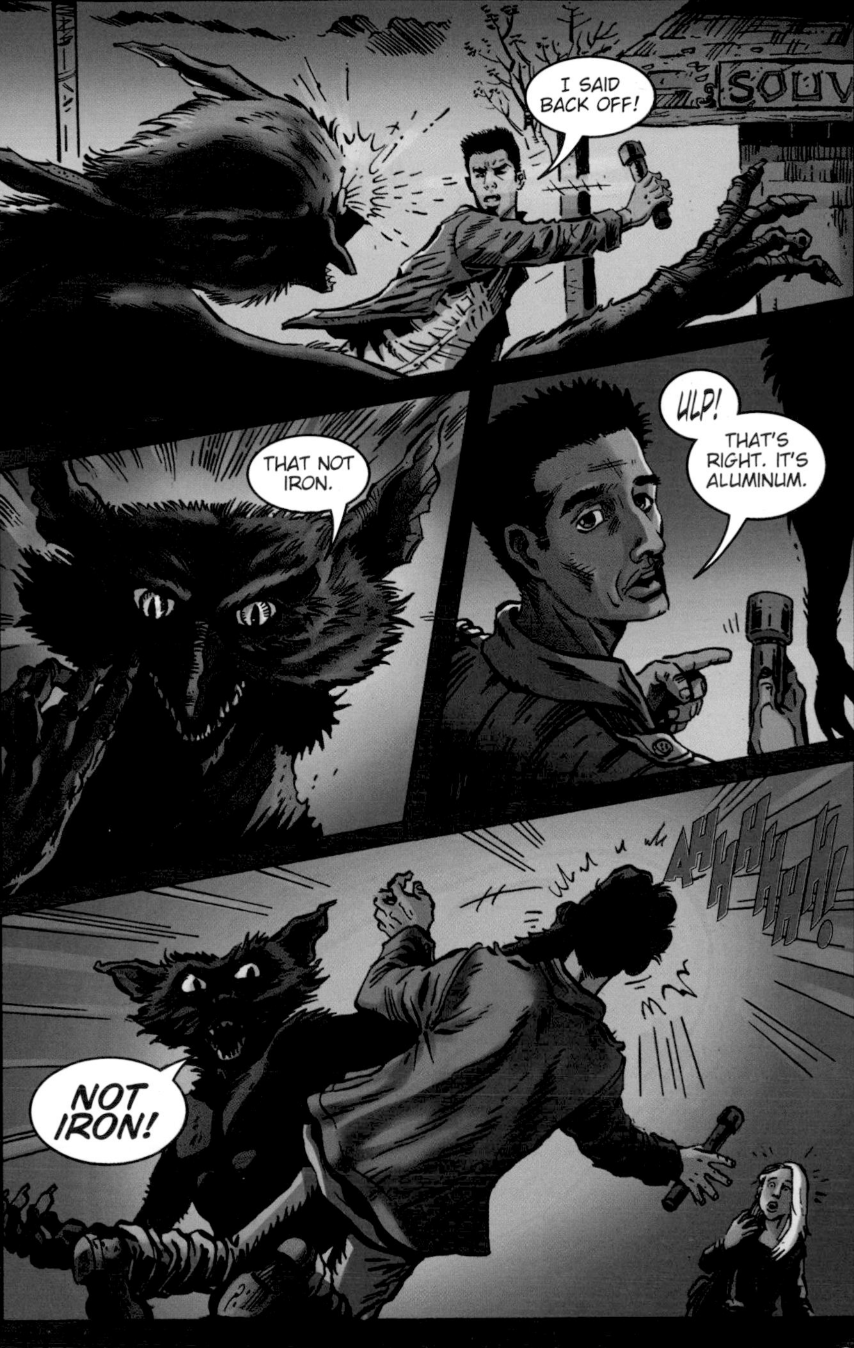
SOUV
I SAID BACK OFF!
THAT NOT IRON.
ULP!
THAT'S RIGHT. IT'S ALUMINUM.
AHHHHHHHH!
NOT IRON!

GO ON TO THE NEXT PAGE.

Rick is in big trouble, but what can you do against a monster like that?

WILL YOU . . .

. . . try to help Rick?
TURN TO PAGE 82.

. . . grab Laura and run?
TURN TO PAGE 69.

As the wheel turns and the basket nears the ground again, you grab onto Laura's collar. She's not very heavy. You think you can drag her along.

"Hey!" shouts Rick. "Let her go!"

"At least I'm going to try something!" you yell back. Then you jump.

For just a second, your feet touch the ground. Then you're dragged back into the air!

Laura's grip on the safety bar was stronger than you thought. She didn't let go. Now your fingers are stuck in her collar. You're being pulled higher and higher.

The basket starts rocking crazily from your weight as you hang off the back. You struggle to hold on, but finally, you lose your grip and plummet to the ground!

THE END

"Laura's right!" you yell to the others. "We all saw the track just a second ago. It must be a trick—an illusion!"

"But I can *see* that it's *gone!*" Rick whimpers.

Just like that, a thought pops into your head. "Close your eyes! If it isn't real and we can't see it, it can't hurt us!"

"T-that's crazy!" says Laura. Still, she closes her eyes tightly and puts her hands over her ears too.

"But—"

"Shut up and do it, Rick! There's no time to argue!"

Then you shut your eyes and clamp your hands over your ears, trying to drown out the sound of the wind and the rattling wheels on the track.

Seconds pass . . . a minute . . .

GO ON TO THE NEXT PAGE.

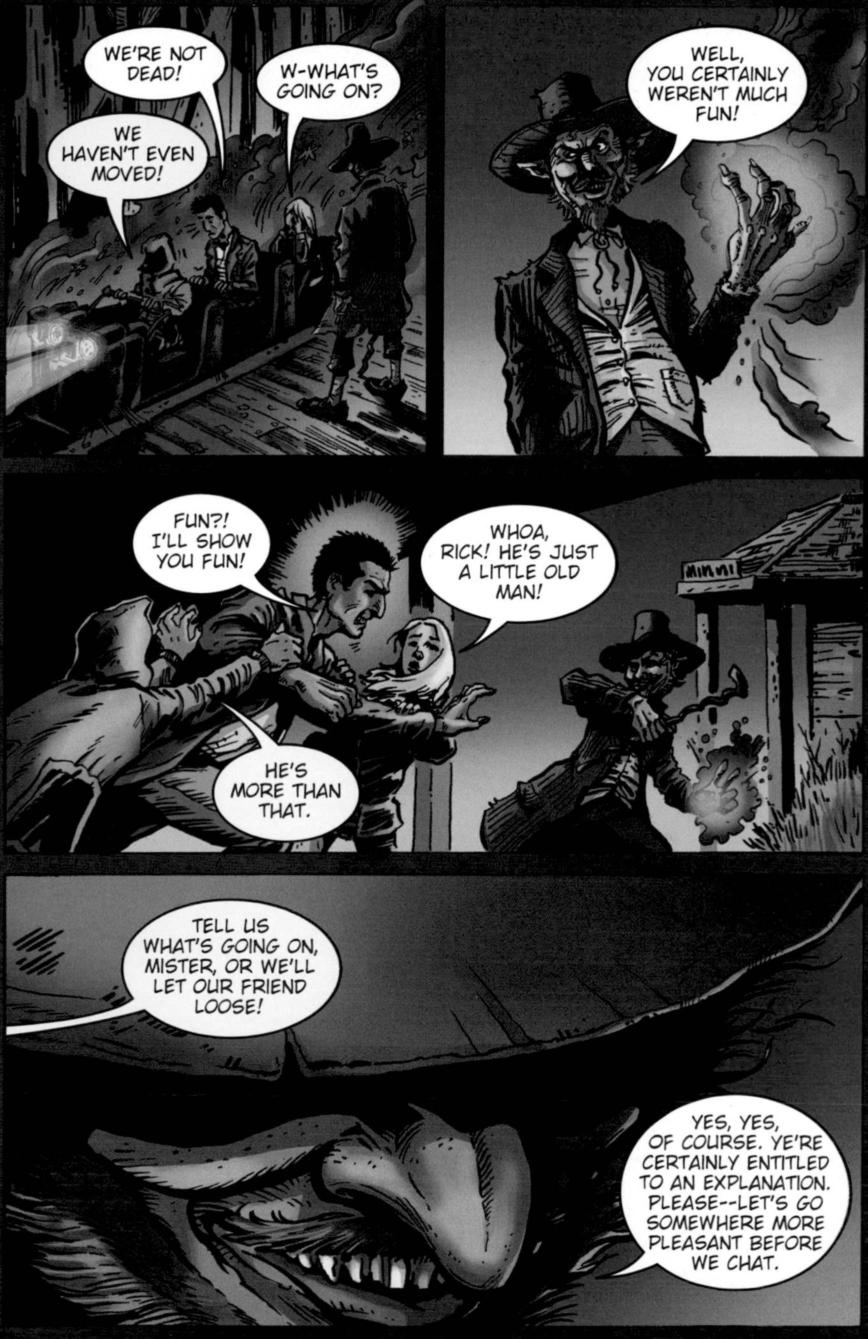
WE'RE NOT DEAD!
WE HAVEN'T EVEN MOVED!
W-WHAT'S GOING ON?
WELL, YOU CERTAINLY WEREN'T MUCH FUN!
FUN?! I'LL SHOW YOU FUN!
WHOA, RICK! HE'S JUST A LITTLE OLD MAN!
HE'S MORE THAN THAT.
TELL US WHAT'S GOING ON, MISTER, OR WE'LL LET OUR FRIEND LOOSE!
YES, YES, OF COURSE. YE'RE CERTAINLY ENTITLED TO AN EXPLANATION. PLEASE--LET'S GO SOMEWHERE MORE PLEASANT BEFORE WE CHAT.

GO ON TO THE NEXT PAGE.

You wonder if it's safe to let him lead you somewhere after the trick he just played on you.

WILL YOU . . .

. . . demand an explanation right then, right there?

TURN TO PAGE 30.

. . . let him take you someplace more pleasant first?

TURN TO PAGE 19.

You and Rick slowly approach the Black Dog. It crouches, growling. Its head swings back and forth, looking at you, then at Rick.

Your hands shake as you struggle to rip open the plastic bag full of salt. Suddenly, it gives way! The plastic comes apart in a salt explosion.

Dropping to your knees, you try to gather it up and form it into a circle around you. A nasty chuckle sounds nearby.

You look up. The Far Darrig is there, sneering at you. "Quite the mess ye've made. That won't help ye at all!"

He raises his gnarled walking stick high and brings it whistling down toward you.

Then everything goes black.

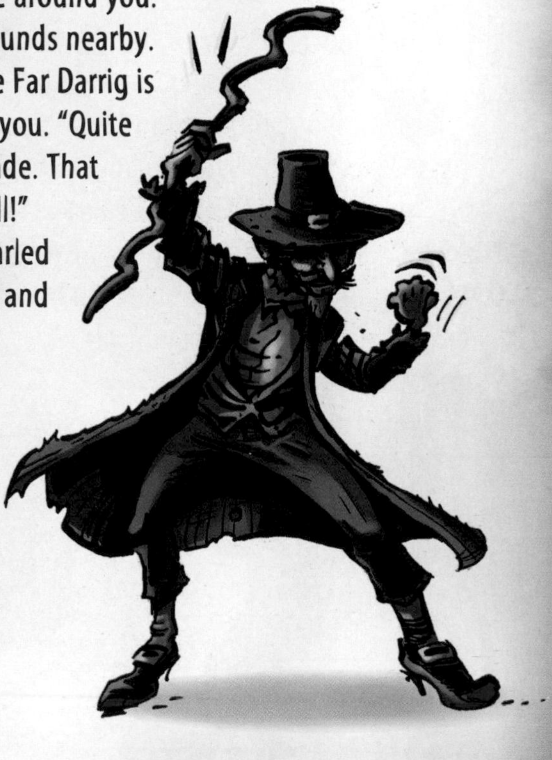

THE END

You take a good look at the old guy and yell, "Run! He'll never catch us!" Laura hesitates, but Rick grabs her arm and drags her along.

As you duck between the ring toss booth and the shooting gallery, you hear the old man's gravelly voice calling out.

"Ye may outrun me," he cries, "but surely my wee pup'll find ye!"

A loud howl echoes through the park. You can't tell if it came from behind you or ahead.

Rick, his long legs pumping furiously, catches up and passes you by. "Hurry!" he shouts. "Faster!"

A quick glance shows that Laura is right behind you. Ahead, Rick turns around the corner of a building, heading for the place you left the blanket. You skid around the corner a second later
and . . . crash into Rick.

"Why'd you stop?" you gasp.

Then you see the huge, slavering hound between you and the fence.

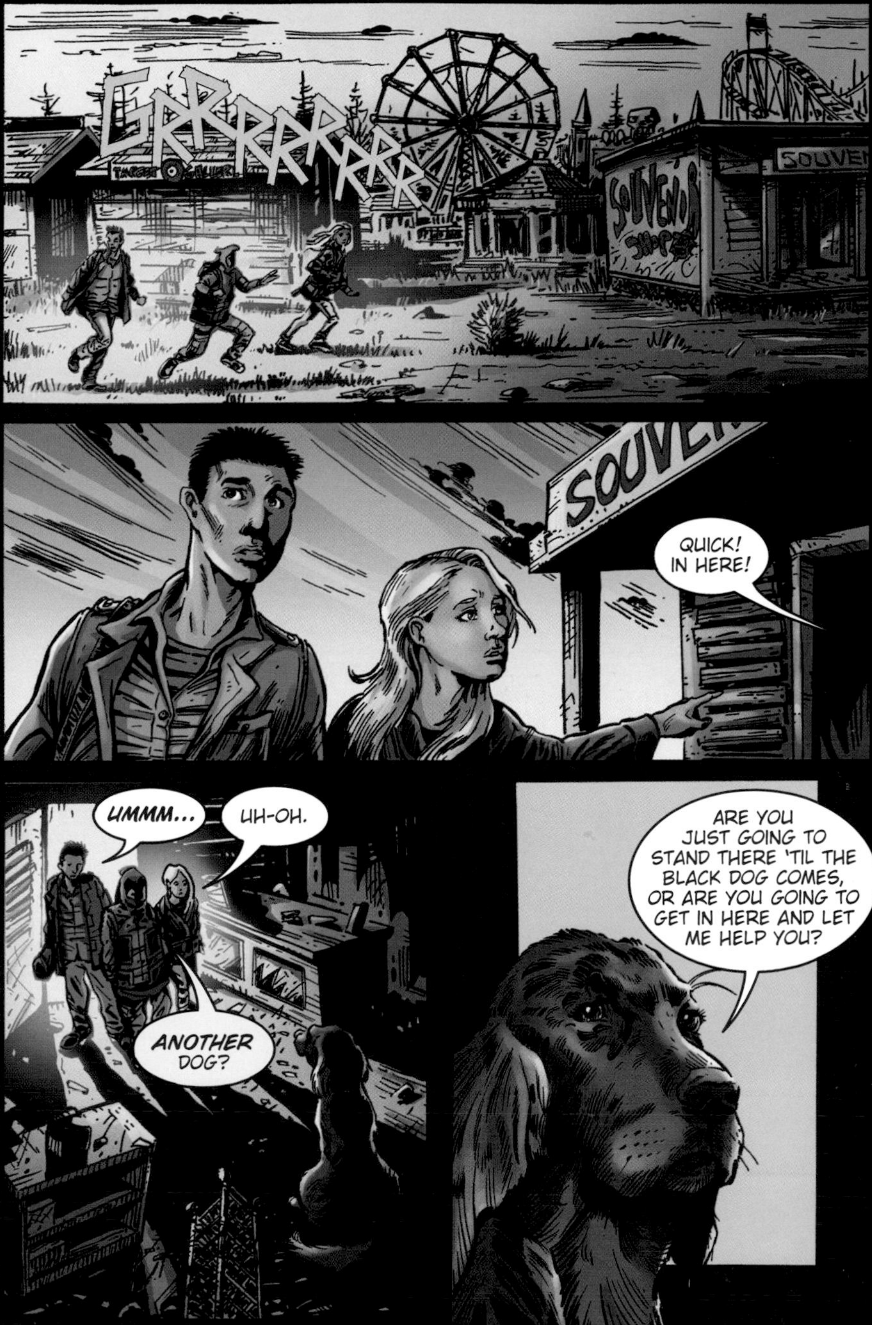
GRRRRRRRR
TARGET GALLERY
SOUVENIR SHOP
SOUVEN
SOUVEN
QUICK! IN HERE!
UMMM...
UH-OH.
ANOTHER DOG?
ARE YOU JUST GOING TO STAND THERE 'TIL THE BLACK DOG COMES, OR ARE YOU GOING TO GET IN HERE AND LET ME HELP YOU?

GO ON TO THE NEXT PAGE.

TWISTED JOURNEYS®

A talking dog! A very big talking dog!

WILL YOU . . .

. . . go inside?
TURN TO PAGE 26.

. . . run away, in case this is some kind of trap?
TURN TO PAGE 94.

"Fine," you say. "We can go someplace nicer, but it better be close!"

The red man bobs his head and smiles. A short walk later, you reach a building with pictures of a bearded woman, a man so thin you can see almost every bone, and a little person.

Laura frowns. "You call this place 'more pleasant'?"

"I do," the red man replies. "Come along."

Inside, glass cases show off animal oddities in jars of formaldehyde: two-headed snakes, frogs with extra legs, a rabbit with no legs, and worse.

There are also a half dozen weird, feather-headed . . . things standing around the room. Each has one arm, one leg, one eye, and a very, very wide mouth. You're glad the eyes and mouths are closed. They're ugly enough as they are.

"What are those things?" you ask.

"Those? They're my friends the fachen!" His smile turns ugly. "Fresh meat, boys!"

As he says that, a half dozen yellow eyes pop open and six huge mouths full of nasty, jagged teeth gape wide.

"I should have mentioned," the red man explains, "when I said 'more pleasant,' I meant for me and my friends."

THE END

You stand firm. "Rick's right. We need to know what's going on."

The dog growls in frustration. "Fine. That wrinkled runt that's hunting you? He's a Far Darrig. His kind delight in tormenting you mortals."

"Us mortals?" asks Laura.

"A bunch of my folk settled in Irish Hills long, long ago," says the dog. "When Summerland was built, we gathered here. We like to do mischief to your kind. The Far Darrig most of all. He accidentally scared a man to death. He found he liked killing. He kept doing it."

"But—" Laura begins.

The dog keeps talking. "Eventually the park's owner trapped us here. I—"

Suddenly its ears prick up. "Sorry," the dog says. "The Far Darrig and his crew are close. I told you we had no time for questions."

"But . . ."

Racing for the back door, the dog barks, "He'll have spriggans with him. Savage creatures. If you've got any iron, now would be a good time to use it!"

GO ON TO THE NEXT PAGE.

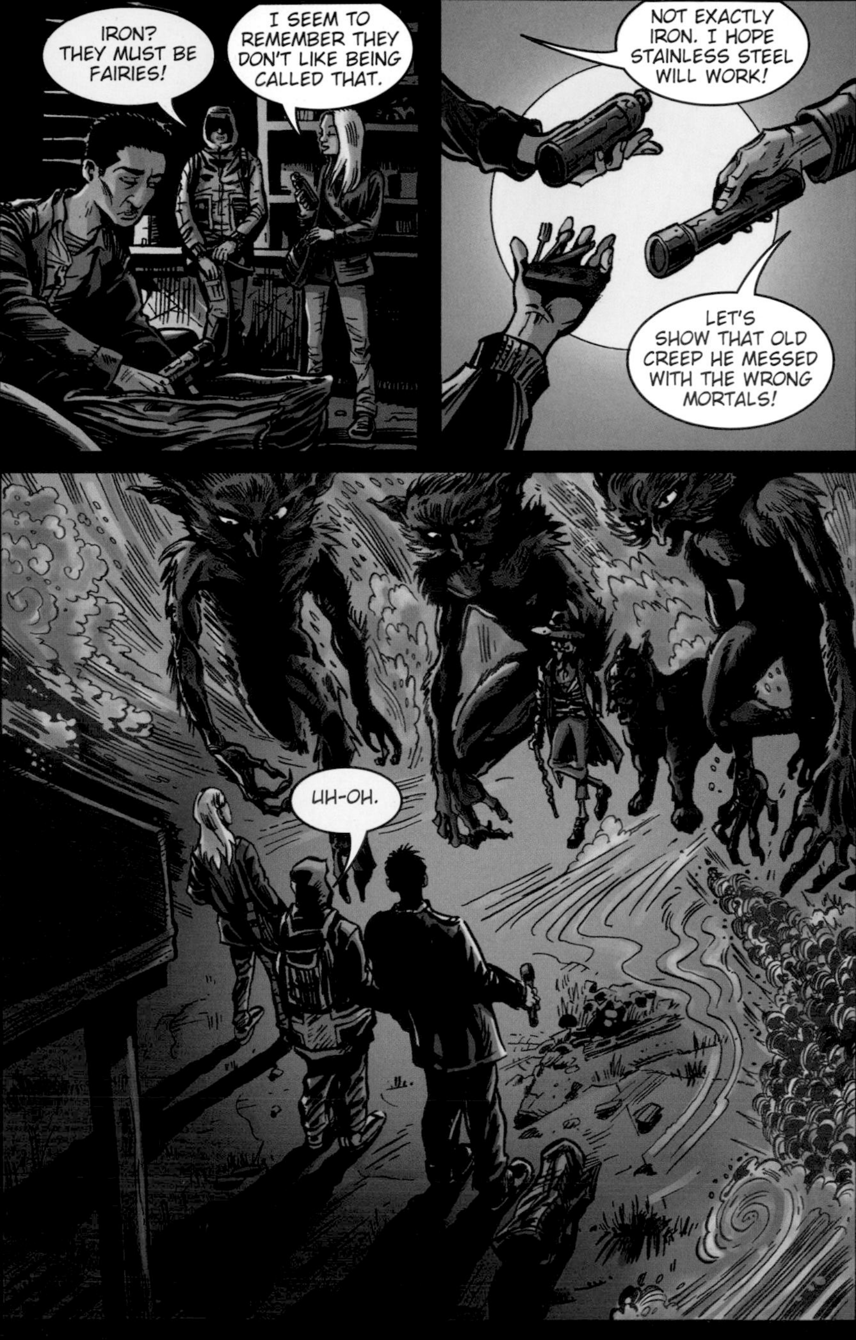
IRON? THEY MUST BE FAIRIES!
I SEEM TO REMEMBER THEY DON'T LIKE BEING CALLED THAT.
NOT EXACTLY IRON. I HOPE STAINLESS STEEL WILL WORK!
LET'S SHOW THAT OLD CREEP HE MESSED WITH THE WRONG MORTALS!
UH-OH.

GO ON TO THE NEXT PAGE.

These things look pretty dangerous.

WILL YOU . . .

. . . rely on your weapons and face down the fairies?
TURN TO PAGE 8.

. . . go back inside and barricade the door?
TURN TO PAGE 25.

Laura insists on dragging you and Rick to the carousel.

"It's a kiddie ride," you complain.

"But carousels are beautiful!" Laura says. "The lights, the brightly painted horses, the music. Don't be such a grump!"

Rick doesn't say anything. He usually goes along with whatever Laura wants.

When you get to the carousel, you have to admit it's impressive. The carousel horses look wild and lifelike. The blaze of lights reflects off the big pond nearby.

Laura points out a silver gray horse and says, "I have to ride that one!" Then she runs on ahead.

"I do like an enthusiastic customer," laughs the Barker. "Hurry up, you two. Pick out horses for yourselves! We don't want to keep your friend waiting!"

"All it does is go in a circle," you mutter. "What's the big deal?"

The carousel might be dull, but standing all by yourself isn't going to be much better.

WILL YOU . . .

. . . wait for the ride to finish up?
TURN TO PAGE 66.

. . . go ahead and ride with Laura and Rick?
TURN TO PAGE 34.

You decide there are too many of them.

"Inside!" you cry as you drag your friends back through the doorway. Slamming the door shut, you look desperately around the room.

"Grab some racks! Block the door!"

You put your back to the door, bracing it, until your friends push the first rack into place.

The three of you pile up more racks and shelves, exchanging nervous looks.

"Why aren't they trying to break down the door?" Laura wonders.

You start to reply, but a loud creaking interrupts you. Looking around, you notice dust drifting down from the rafters.

Rick notices it too. "What the—?"

Then you hear the cracking and splintering of wood.

"They're not trying to break down the door!" you scream. "They're knocking down the building!"

That's when the walls collapse and the ceiling comes crashing down.

THE END

With a shrug, you scoot inside. At least this dog seems friendly. Rick and Laura hesitate, but you urge them on.

The dog starts trotting toward the back of the shop. Rick scowls. "Wait a second! What's going on here?"

"We don't really have time for questions," the dog replies. "I'm doing what I can to mask your scent, but that won't keep the Black Dog busy for long."

"Who . . . what . . . are you?" you ask.

The dog grins. "You can call me Setter. Now come along."

As you follow it through the door into a dusty storeroom, it asks, "And what are you called, then?"

"The skyscraper is Rick," Laura replies. "I'm Laura and that's—"

"Look," says Rick, "I don't think we should be the ones answering questions here. I want to know what kind of crazy is going on!"

"Starting with how a dog can talk," you say.

GO ON TO THE NEXT PAGE.

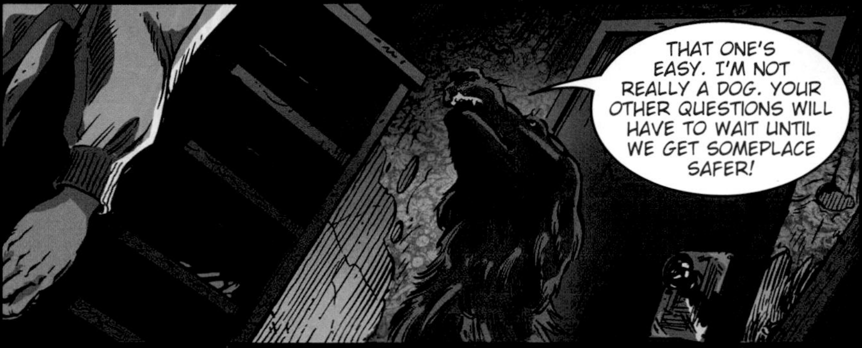
THAT ONE'S EASY. I'M NOT REALLY A DOG. YOUR OTHER QUESTIONS WILL HAVE TO WAIT UNTIL WE GET SOMEPLACE SAFER!

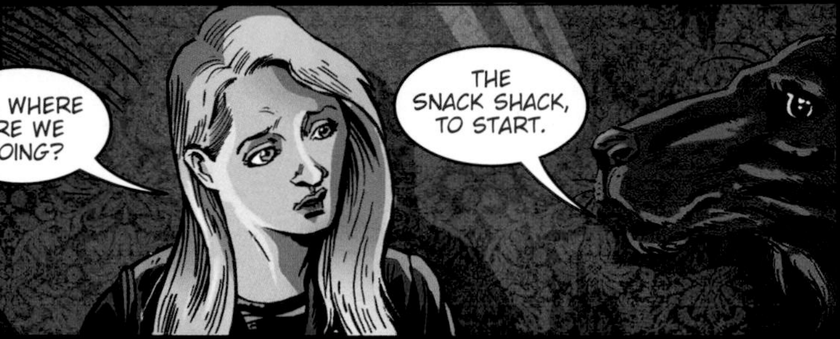
SO, WHERE ARE WE GOING?
THE SNACK SHACK, TO START.

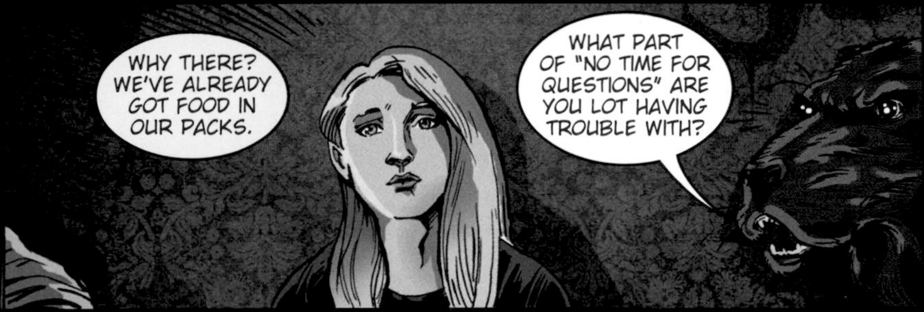
WHY THERE? WE'VE ALREADY GOT FOOD IN OUR PACKS.
WHAT PART OF "NO TIME FOR QUESTIONS" ARE YOU LOT HAVING TROUBLE WITH?

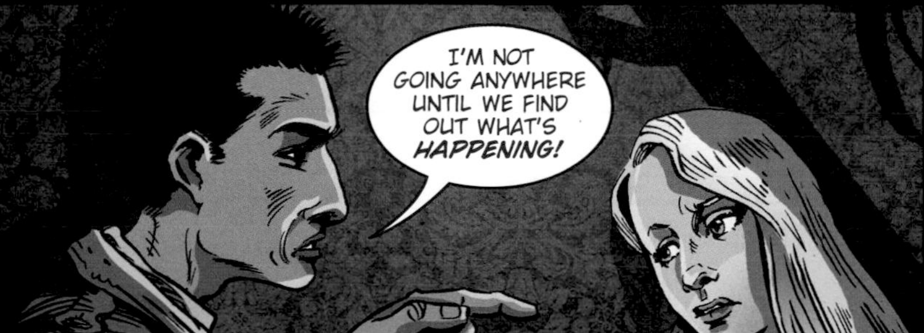
I'M NOT GOING ANYWHERE UNTIL WE FIND OUT WHAT'S *HAPPENING!*

GO ON TO THE NEXT PAGE.

WILL YOU . . .

. . . tell Rick that the answers can wait?

TURN TO PAGE 89.

. . . insist that Setter explain what's happening?

TURN TO PAGE 20.

"Better than nothing," you say.

You and Rick start *plink*ing away. You scream like maniacs too, hoping that will scare the animals.

When the first BB hits the lion, a puff of what looks like colored smoke come out of it. You keep firing and the thing finally disappears entirely!

Rick takes care of the water buffalo and the cheetah. The two of you turn your BB guns on the elephant before it can trample Laura. The monstrosity vanishes.

"What is going on?" Laura asks.

Rick turns toward the Barker.

"Start talking," Rick says.

The Barker gives a nervous laugh. "Or else what? All you have is a BB gun. How can you hurt me?"

"Worked pretty well on those animals," you say.

The Barker gulps.

TURN TO PAGE 77.

29

"This seems pleasant enough to me," you growl.

The little red man lets out a long sigh.

"Very well," he says. "My folk and I have lived here in the Irish Hills for as long as they've been known as the Irish Hills. We were peaceful and content, doing small favors for nice mortal folk from time to time.

"But a cruel man went and put this park right on top of our home! Is it any wonder we fought back?"

"Wait," you say, "is that why the park had a reputation for accidents? You and your folk . . . ?"

The red man nods. "We wanted to drive everyone away. And we did! But the cruel man shut us in here with that terrible fence and a circle of rowan trees our folk cannot cross. After what your kind did to mine, can ye blame me for having a little fun at your expense?"

"Are there any more of your kind still around?" Laura asks.

The red man smiles a big crooked grin. "There are! Would ye like to meet 'em?"

GO ON TO THE NEXT PAGE.

FROM WHAT HE'S SAID, YOU'RE PRETTY SURE *HIS KIND* ARE FAIRIES! FROM THE STORIES YOU'VE READ, THAT MEANS YOU PROBABLY CAN'T TRUST HIM.

I THINK WE SHOULD GET OUT OF HERE BEFORE YOU HAVE ANY MORE FUN AT OUR EXPENSE.

YOU THINK YOU REMEMBER READING SOMETHING ELSE ABOUT FAIRIES TOO...

WELL THEN, BE OFF WITH YOU AND I'LL BE ON MY WAY.

LET ME SHOW YOU SOMETHING FIRST!

ULP! IS THAT...?

YES. WELL, STEEL, BUT YOU PROBABLY WON'T LIKE THAT ANY BETTER.

WHY DON'T YOU COME TO THE FENCE WITH US? THAT WAY YOU CAN TELL ANY OF YOUR FRIENDS WE MEET TO LEAVE US BE.

YES! OF COURSE! THIS WAY!

WITH YOUR 'ESCORT' IT DOESN'T TAKE TOO LONG BEFORE YOU'RE OVER THE FENCE AND ON YOUR WAY HOME!

Thanks FOR VISITING COME BACK SOON!

THE END

Laura makes a good point,
but Setter is helping you escape.

WILL YOU . . .

. . . help Setter escape from the park?
TURN TO PAGE 39.

. . . say no, since she admitted to hurting humans?
TURN TO PAGE 52.

"I don't think so," you say.

"Why not?" asks Rick.

"He already tried to run us over with an elephant."

"Just an illusion," the red man puts in.

You glare at him. "I'd rather not risk it. Let's just go."

Laura nods.

"So I put a little scare in ye," says the red man. "I also showed ye the park in all its glory! Ungrateful wretches! Fine, I'll be on my way."

You step in front of him before he can walk away. Rick stands behind him. "How about you walk us to the fence?" you ask. "Since we're friends and all?"

He isn't happy about it, but he agrees.

Before long, you're at the spot where you first came in. Laura throws the blanket over the barbed wire and scrambles over it while you and Rick watch the red man. Then you both scramble over it. Fast!

As you climb into the SUV, the red man snarls through the fence, "Come back again soon."

You don't think you will.

THE END

Eventually, you let your friends convince you to join them on the carousel. It's a kiddie ride, but some of the horses *do* look pretty cool.

You pick one that's bigger than the rest, jet black with red eyes. It looks wicked! Once you've all mounted up, Laura asks the Barker when the ride's going to start.

"Right now," he laughs.

Suddenly something doesn't feel right. The carousel horse feels colder. Like it's wet. Then something shifts beneath you. As if the horse is getting bigger!

The next thing you know, you find yourself perched on top of a wild-eyed, living horse. Its black coat drips cold, stinking water.

You look over at your friends. Their horses have changed too!

"What's going on?!" you scream.

"You didn't want to go on a kiddie ride," says the Barker as he tips his hat in your direction. "The Each Uisge definitely isn't that!"

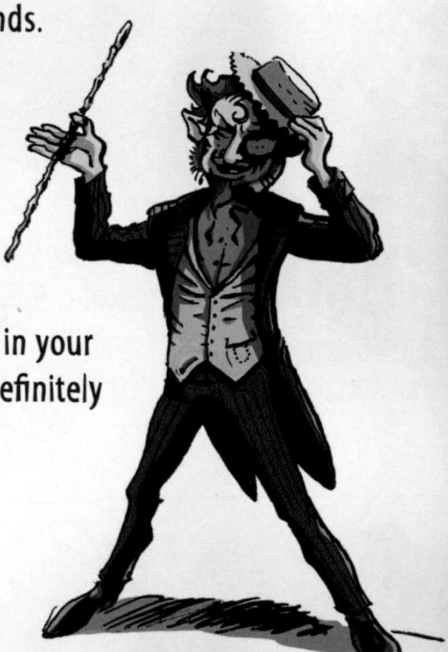

GO ON TO THE NEXT PAGE.

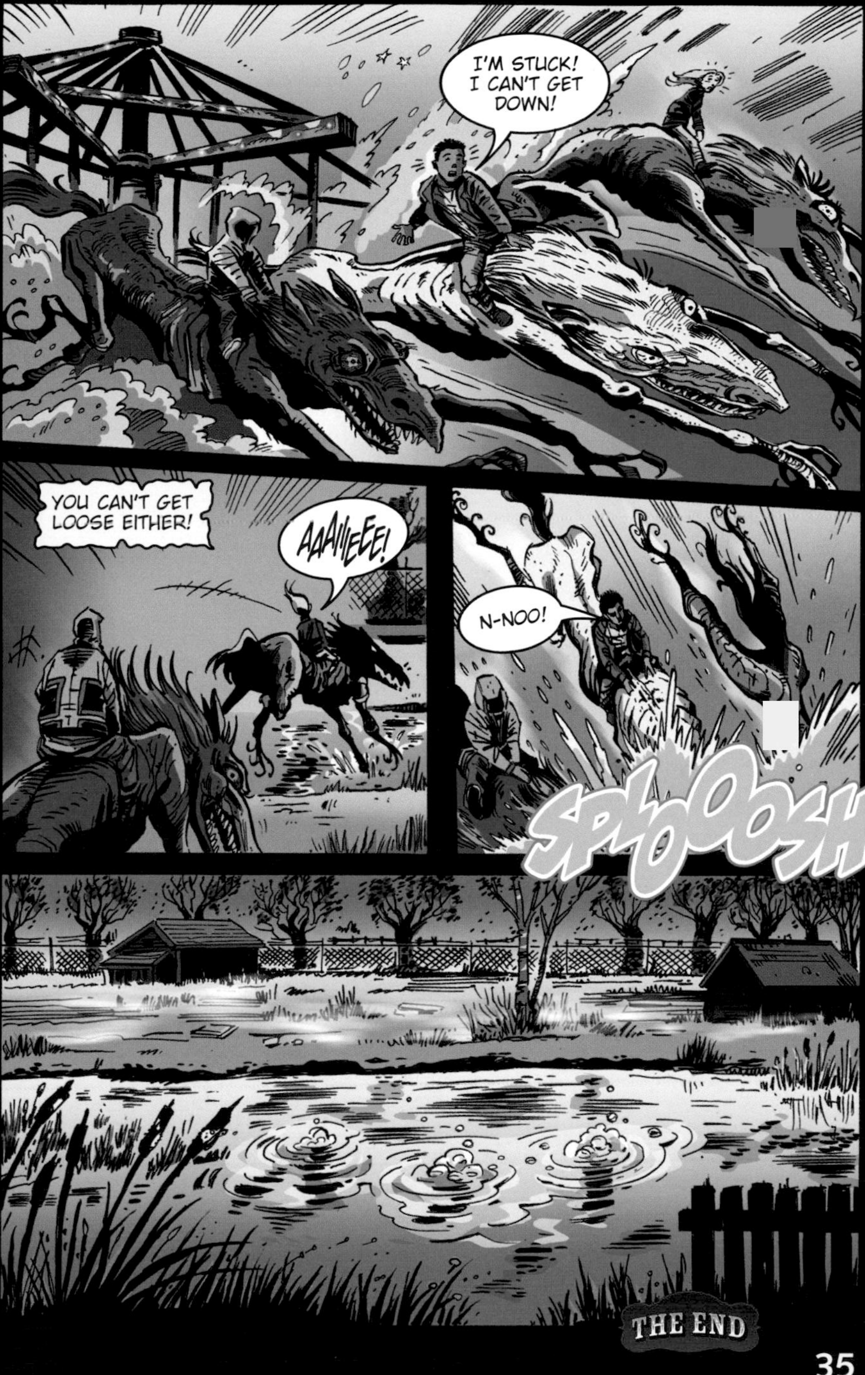
I'M STUCK! I CAN'T GET DOWN!
YOU CAN'T GET LOOSE EITHER!
AAAIIEEE!
N-NOO!
SPLOOOSH
THE END

When you get to the Ferris wheel, the Barker asks if you're sure you don't want to start with something more exciting.

"No, this is good!" Rick says.

"All right, then," says the Barker. "As you say, quite a view. And it may serve."

"Serve for what?" you ask.

He looks surprised. "Eh? Oh, sorry. Just thinking aloud. Pay me no mind."

As you get ready to climb into a basket on the Ferris wheel, Rick looks over at another attraction and smiles.

"Wait a second," he says, "why don't we try that one first?"

He's pointing at the Tunnel of Love.

"I thought you wanted to do the Ferris wheel first," Laura says.

He gives her a nervous smile. "I can wait," he says. "If you want to . . . y'know . . . go there first."

She blushes and says, "That might be nice."

GO ON TO THE NEXT PAGE.

TWISTED JOURNEYS®

You can't help rolling your eyes, but the two of
them want to do the Tunnel of Love now.

WILL YOU . . .

. . . push for the Ferris wheel?
TURN TO PAGE 61.

. . . agree to the Tunnel of Love?
TURN TO PAGE 72.

Laura wants to go back for the car. You agree.

However, once you get to the SUV, you realize that Rick had the keys.

"Guess we'll have to walk," you say.

As you reach the end of the drive, you hear a voice behind you: "Well, well, looks like we meet again!"

You turn to see the red man leaning against the stone posts that hold up the Summerland sign.

"You can't hurt us!" Laura says. "You promised!"

"I swore you would leave Summerland unharmed." He glances up at the sign. "It seems you've done that."

He grins wickedly and gives the stone pillar a gentle pat. It crumbles as if it were hit by a wrecking ball. With a metallic moan, the sign dips forward.

The last thing you see as the sign crashes down on you is the evil smile on the little red man's face.

THE END

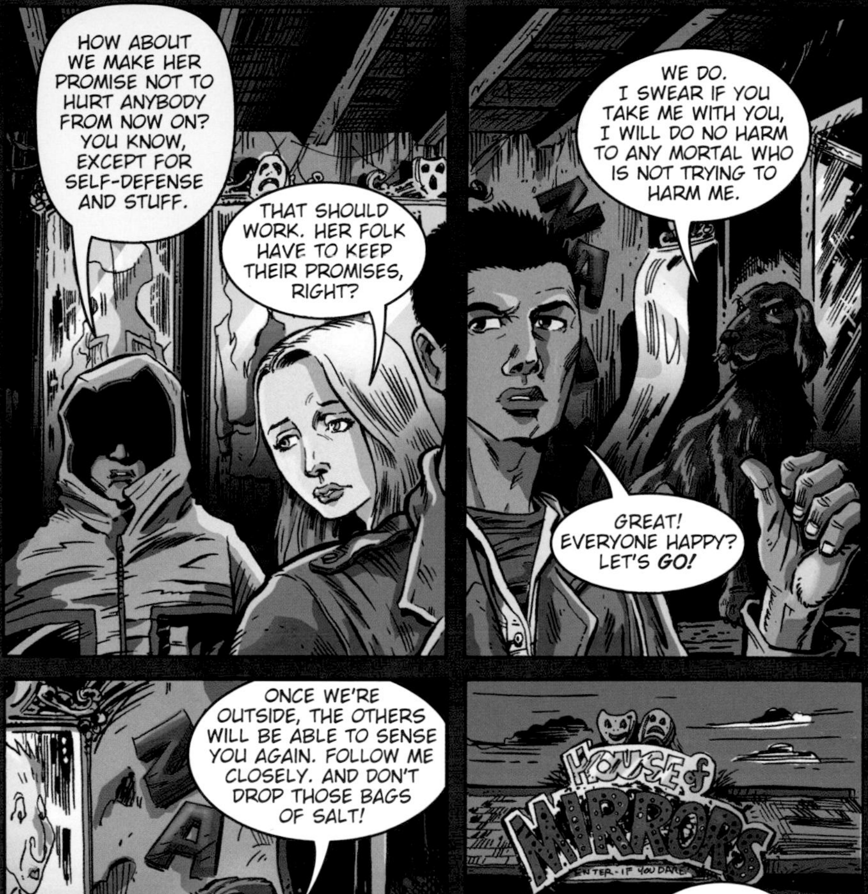

HOW ABOUT WE MAKE HER PROMISE NOT TO HURT ANYBODY FROM NOW ON? YOU KNOW, EXCEPT FOR SELF-DEFENSE AND STUFF.
THAT SHOULD WORK. HER FOLK HAVE TO KEEP THEIR PROMISES, RIGHT?
WE DO. I SWEAR IF YOU TAKE ME WITH YOU, I WILL DO NO HARM TO ANY MORTAL WHO IS NOT TRYING TO HARM ME.
GREAT! EVERYONE HAPPY? LET'S ***GO!***
ONCE WE'RE OUTSIDE, THE OTHERS WILL BE ABLE TO SENSE YOU AGAIN. FOLLOW ME CLOSELY. AND DON'T DROP THOSE BAGS OF SALT!
HOUSE of MIRRORS
ENTER - IF YOU DARE
QUICKLY NOW! IT ISN'T FAR!
SALT
BE SHORT!

GO ON TO THE NEXT PAGE.

Just as you glimpse the fence, a high-pitched voice shouts from somewhere above you.

"Over here! The pooka is with them!"

Looking up, you see a tiny man, barely ten inches tall, with dragonfly wings and a tiny bow and quiver. He lets out a shrill, impossibly loud whistle.

A deep, dreadful howling answers him. You're sure it's the Black Dog! You run even faster.

The four of you reach the fence. Setter barks, "The salt! Quickly! Pour out a semicircle around us so that we may climb safely!"

You tear at the bag you're holding, as the winged man swoops down toward you.

Rick drops his bag and starts to climb. "Forget it! We're home free!"

You point toward the little archer above you. A swarm of others aren't far behind. "What about them?"

"What about them?" laughs Rick. "What're those shrimps going to do to someone our size?"

Maybe Rick is right. What harm
can a tiny arrow do?

WILL YOU . . .

. . . take the time to spread the salt?
TURN TO PAGE 68.

. . . follow Rick's lead and climb?
TURN TO PAGE 45.

"Rick's right! We've got the salt. We should just head for the fence!"

The pooka just shakes her head. "Good luck with that."

As Rick opens the door and looks around, Laura gives Setter a quick hug. "Thanks for helping us."

"No need to thank me. You'll never make it."

You grin. "We'll make it all right!"

The three of you sprint toward the fence and safety. You can hear noises in the distance, but you're sure that no one is close by.

Then a huge, dark shape slams into Laura, knocking her flat.

You and Rick skid to a stop.

GO ON TO THE NEXT PAGE.

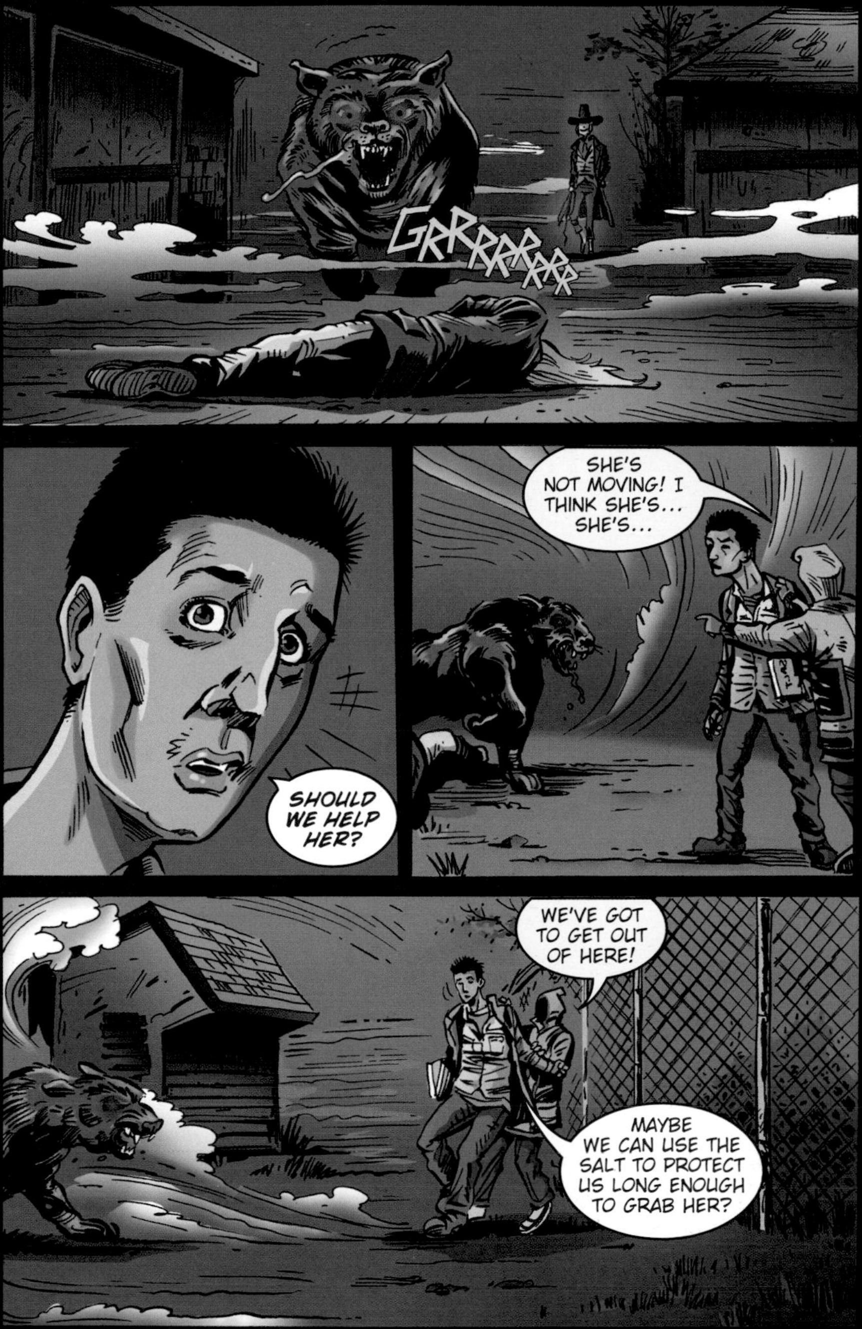
GRRRRRRRR
SHOULD WE HELP HER?
SHE'S NOT MOVING! I THINK SHE'S... SHE'S...
WE'VE GOT TO GET OUT OF HERE!
MAYBE WE CAN USE THE SALT TO PROTECT US LONG ENOUGH TO GRAB HER?

Laura is your friend, but that dog is really vicious.

WILL YOU . . .

. . . make a break for the fence?
TURN TO PAGE 59.

. . . help Rick get Laura?
TURN TO PAGE 15.

"He's right," you say to Laura. "Getting hit with an arrow that size? Like a pinprick!"

You drop your bag of salt and start climbing after Rick. Out of the corner of your eye, you see Setter turn from a dog into a red-feathered eagle and take flight.

"I tried!" Setter cries. "You're on your own!"

You hear a buzzing noise and look up. Rick is perched atop the fence. Almost free! Then you see a half dozen tiny arrows sticking out of his neck and cheek. He tumbles back to the ground, completely limp.

Suddenly, you feel a sharp pain in your hand. It feels like a bee sting, but only for a second. Then your hand goes numb.

You lose your grip on the fence and fall to the ground. At least you think you do. From that moment on, you can't feel anything at all.

THE END

"We're really sorry, mister. We thought the park was abandoned. We didn't think anyone would mind us poking around."

He glares back. "Never thought someone might still be hauntin' the old place, eh?"

At the word *haunting*, you, Rick, and Laura exchange nervous glances. "We're . . . um . . . amusement park buffs. Love these places! And, you know, Summerland is famous."

The old man gives a dry chuckle. "Infamous, you mean."

"No!" you say. "I mean, yes. I mean, we've heard all about it, the good and the bad. We just had to check it out."

Rick decides to join in, trying to flatter the old guy. "You can tell just looking at her that she was a great park! Wish we could have seen her when she was open, all the lights and the sounds and . . . um . . . stuff."

The old man cackles at that. "Oh, ye wish that, do ye? Well now, let's see what I can do."

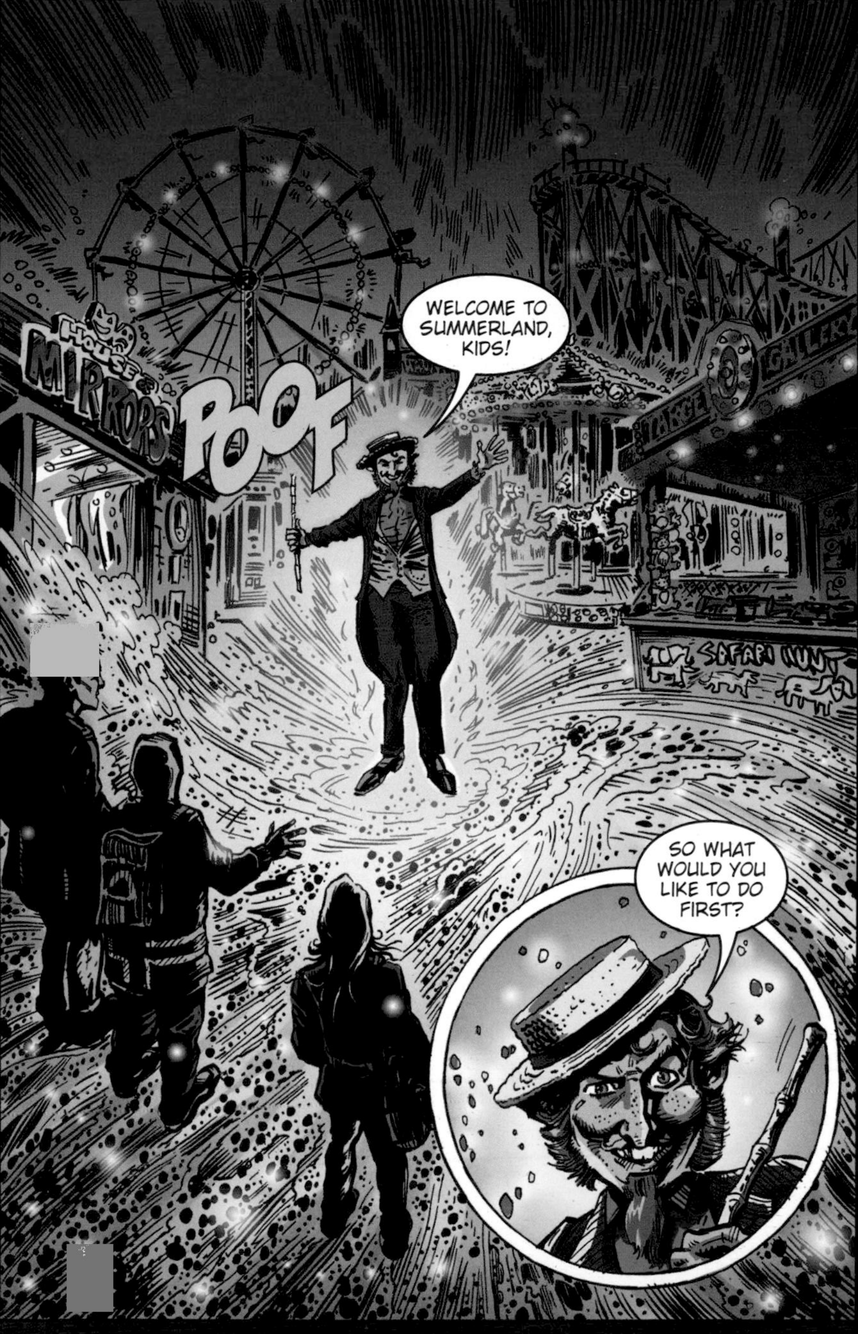
HOUSE OF MIRRORS
POOF
WELCOME TO SUMMERLAND, KIDS!
SAFARI HUNT
SO WHAT WOULD YOU LIKE TO DO FIRST?

It's like magic! You want to go right to the roller coaster. Rick wants to see the view from the Ferris wheel. Laura wants to ride the carousel.

WILL YOU . . .

. . . insist on the coaster first?
TURN TO PAGE 98.

. . . check out the Ferris wheel?
TURN TO PAGE 36.

. . . ride the carousel?
TURN TO PAGE 23.

You rush down to the lakeshore. There's not even a ripple on the surface. Desperate, you dive forward and start swimming. Every few yards, you duck your head under the water, looking for Rick and Laura. But the water is too murky, and there's not enough light. You're as good as blind.

Something brushes your face. Seaweed, you think. It has to be seaweed. Then you feel something slide by you. Something big. Something fast.

You forget about your friends. You struggle upward, fighting against the weight of your wet clothes.

Finally, you reach the surface! You drag air deep into your lungs.

Then something clamps onto your ankle. Your hand clutches for anything to help you from going under, but there's nothing to grab. With a final gasp, you slide back into the lake.

THE END

TOGETHER, YOU AND SETTER CONVINCE RICK AND LAURA TO COME ALONG.

IN HERE! MIRRORS HAVE SPECIAL PROPERTIES. THEY WILL HELP CONFUSE OUR PURSUERS.

MANY OTHER MORTALS HAVE INTRUDED HERE OVER THE YEARS. NONE HAVE EVER ESCAPED.

HEY! YOUR REFLECTION--?

I TOLD YOU I WAS NOT REALLY A DOG.

Y-YOU'RE A GIRL!

MORE OR LESS.

NOW THAT WE HAVE A FEW UNINTERRUPTED MOMENTS TO SPARE, I HAVE A FAVOR TO ASK.

"What?" you ask.

"Normally my sort pays the passing years little attention," Setter says, "but being trapped here has taken its toll. We are weaker than we were. We will grow weaker still. I'll help you escape, but you must take me with you. I cannot pass the fence or rowans myself, but you could carry me."

Rick shrugs. "Sure. Whatever. Let's go."

"Hold on," Laura says to Setter. "You and . . . um . . . the others were locked in here for a reason, right? People died!"

Setter nods. "That's true."

"You mean they're criminals," you say. "That taking Setter with us would be kind of a jail break?"

"I've never killed one of your kind," Setter says.

"But you've hurt people?" Laura asks.

Setter nods.

"At least you're honest," you say.

"My folk do not lie." Setter smiles. "Though we sometimes make the truth confusing."

"I just want to go home," Rick says, miserably.

GO ON TO PAGE 32.

"Sorry, Setter," you say. "You admitted that you've hurt people. We can't set you free."

Strangely, the pooka doesn't seem very upset. "Very well. Let's get you to the fence."

You duck and dodge between buildings and rides. Before long, you're at the fence.

"I guess this is good-bye," Laura says to Setter.

"Perhaps," says the pooka.

As you reach for the fence, it starts to glow. You yank back your hand and turn toward your friends. "It's red hot!"

Setter just grins at you and says quietly, "Perhaps you'll reconsider taking me with you?"

In the distance, you hear the sounds of marching feet and the howling of the Black Dog.

The nasty fairies are getting closer.
WILL YOU . . .

. . . take the pooka with you?
TURN TO PAGE 111.

. . . refuse to be blackmailed?
TURN TO PAGE 71.

"Laura doesn't want to, Rick. Anyway, we can always come back after we ride the coaster!"

"Okay, okay," says Rick. "But we *have* to come back."

A short walk from the shooting gallery brings you to the roller coaster platform. Even though it looks like new, the coaster is an old-style wooden one. Rick looks unimpressed.

"I was hoping for one of those cool vortex coasters," says Rick.

"In a park that's been shut down for twenty years?" you say. "Besides, this kind of coaster shakes and bumps around more. Way scarier!"

"I can promise you that!" says the Barker. He points his cane at the front car and grins. "All aboard!"

Laura drags you into the front seat of the three-seat car. "Let's get going!" she shouts.

"Let's." The Barker grins. Then the cars lurch forward and start groaning their way up the first big hill.

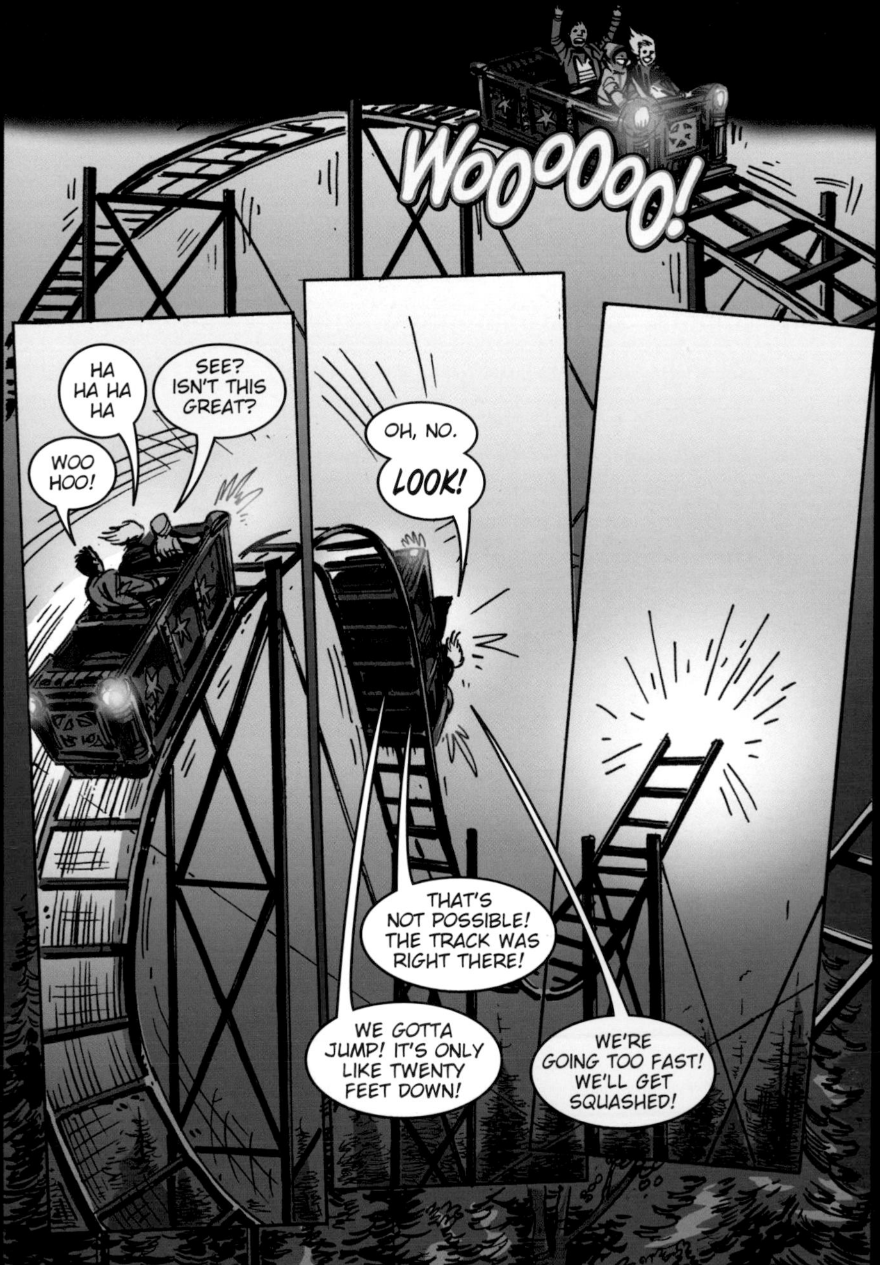
WOOoOOOO!
HA HA HA HA
SEE? ISN'T THIS GREAT?
WOO HOO!
OH, NO.
LOOK!
THAT'S NOT POSSIBLE! THE TRACK WAS RIGHT THERE!
WE GOTTA JUMP! IT'S ONLY LIKE TWENTY FEET DOWN!
WE'RE GOING TOO FAST! WE'LL GET SQUASHED!

GO ON TO THE NEXT PAGE.

It might be safer to jump from the back car onto the tracks. If you can *reach* the back car.

WILL YOU . . .

. . . trust Laura and believe that the track couldn't have just disappeared?

TURN TO PAGE 12.

. . . jump just before the crash like Rick suggests?

TURN TO PAGE 105.

. . . climb to the back car and jump onto the track?

TURN TO PAGE 110.

"Got it!" You lock the wire cutters into place, scramble up the fence, and cut the bottom wire. It parts with a pinging sound.

"This is taking too long," Rick says. He starts to climb up beside you as you work on the second strand.

He has just made it to the top when you hear a whistling noise and a loud thump. Without even a gasp, Rick topples off the fence and falls limply on the other side.

Something small and hard slams into your back. Suddenly, your legs don't want to work. You lose your grip on the fence and tumble off.

As you lie on the ground, your sight going dark, you notice something lying not far from you. Is that . . . a baseball?

You can't help wondering where in the world these monsters got a baseball to throw at you. The last thing you see is the ball rolling away—and the creatures beginning to advance . . .

THE END

Taking deep breaths, you try to calm yourself down.

"You okay?" Rick asks.

"Yeah," you say. "Let's get out of here. Who knows what else that little creep can do?"

The two of you take off for the fence. You don't even bother trying to find where you left the blanket. You just find the section nearest to the roller coaster and climb. You get a few scratches going over the barbed wire. You don't really care.

Rick pauses, staring back through the fence. "What are we going to tell Laura's family?" he asks.

"I don't know," you say, "but let's make sure we live long enough to tell them something. I don't know if that thing can get through the fence, but I don't want to find out."

With that thought, the two of you start running for the car.

THE END

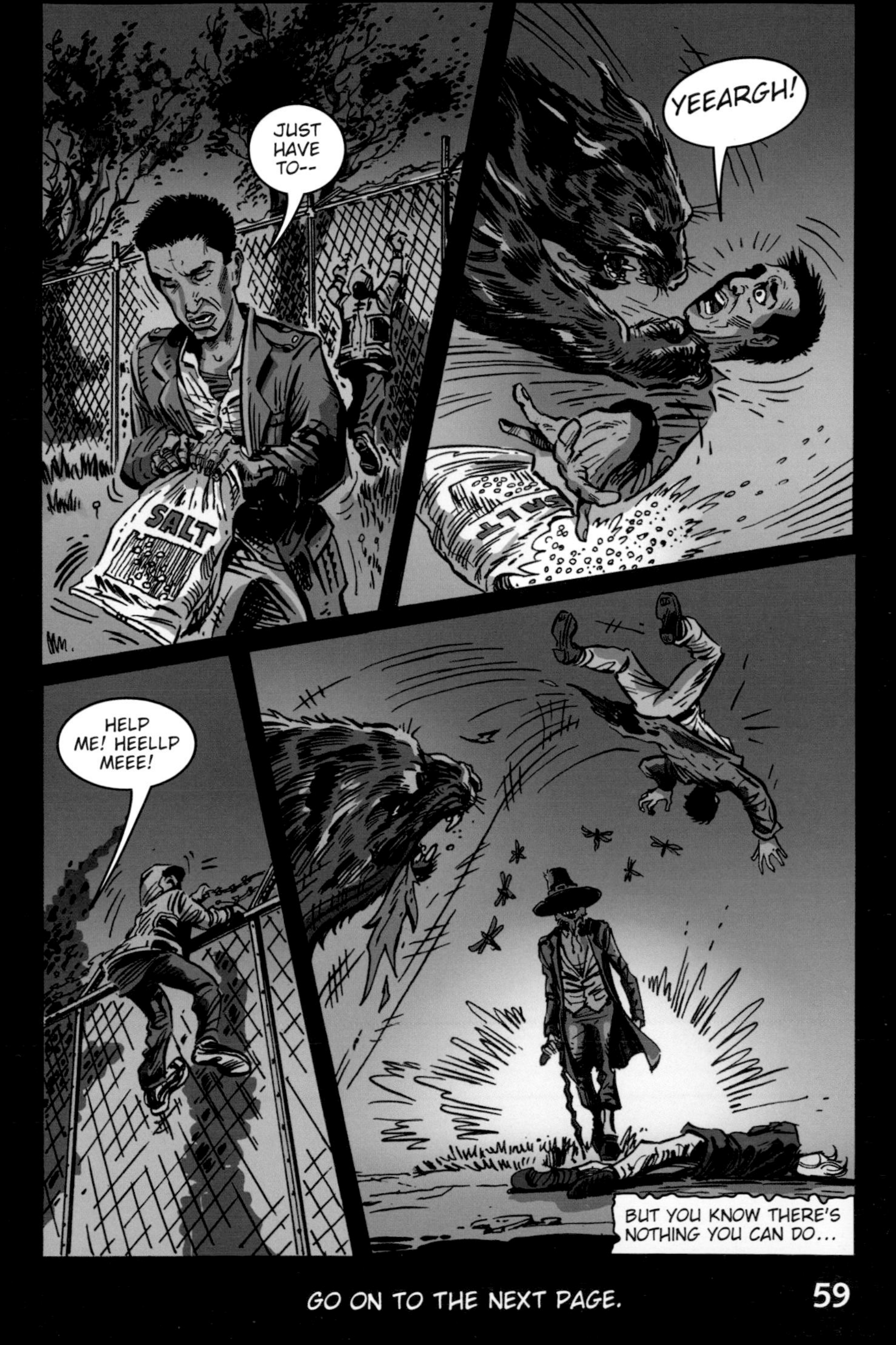
JUST HAVE TO--
SALT
YEEARGH!
HELP ME! HEELLP MEEE!
BUT YOU KNOW THERE'S NOTHING YOU CAN DO...

You leap the strands of barbed wire and drop to the ground. You tumble forward, slamming into the grass.

Gasping for air, you scramble to your feet. You don't even look back. You can't look back. Your friends . . .

You crash through the rowan trees and into the woods beyond. Branches lash at your face as you run. You tell yourself that's why your eyes are tearing up.

You're not sure how long it takes you to reach the road, but when you do, you keep running. Eventually, you can't run anymore. You stumble and fall.

As you lie by the roadside, gulping air into your burning lungs, you realize that you left everything behind at Summerland. The truck, your friends—and maybe your sanity.

THE END

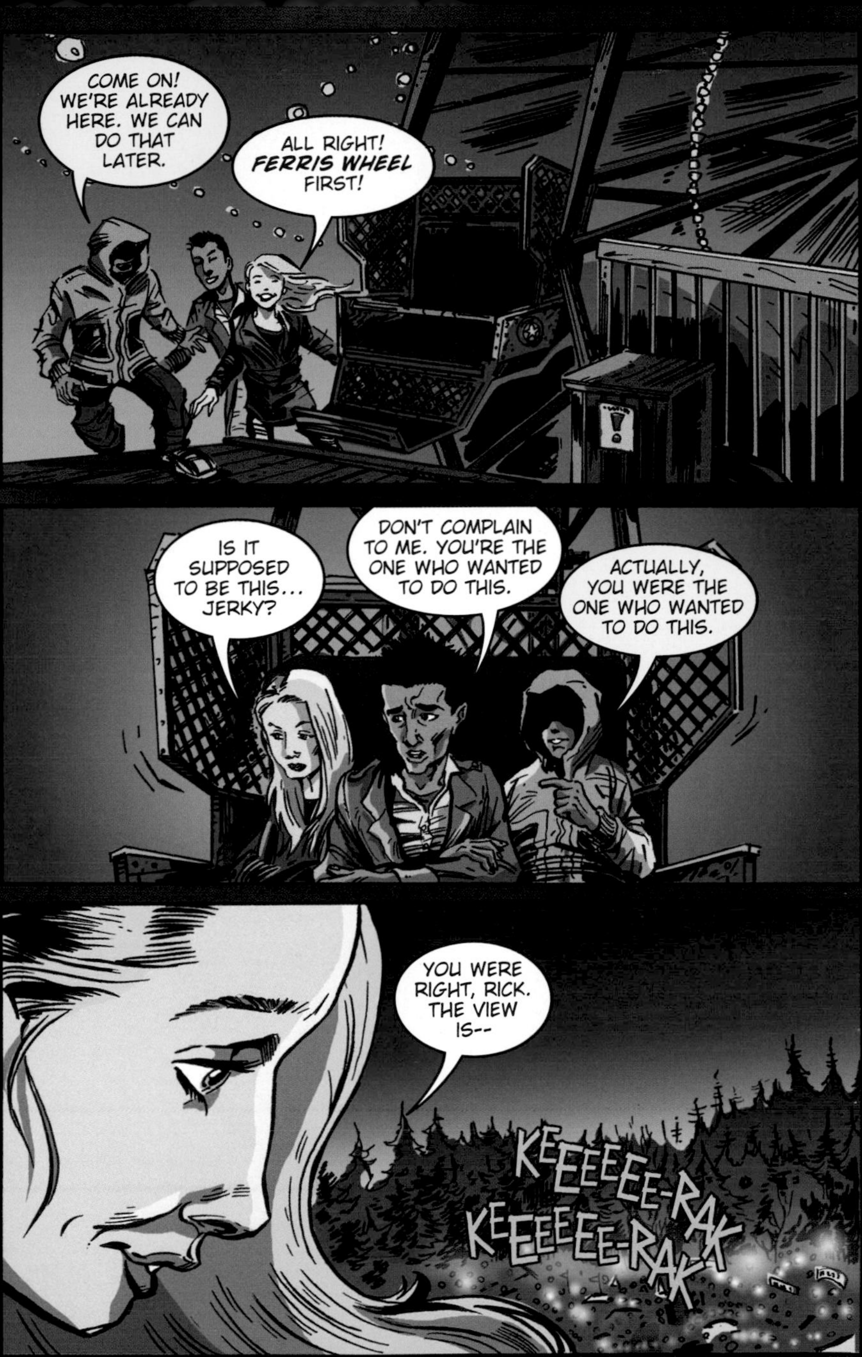
COME ON! WE'RE ALREADY HERE. WE CAN DO THAT LATER.
ALL RIGHT! **FERRIS WHEEL** FIRST!
IS IT SUPPOSED TO BE THIS... JERKY?
DON'T COMPLAIN TO ME. YOU'RE THE ONE WHO WANTED TO DO THIS.
ACTUALLY, YOU WERE THE ONE WHO WANTED TO DO THIS.
YOU WERE RIGHT, RICK. THE VIEW IS--
KEEEEEE-RAK
KEEEEEE-RAK

GO ON TO THE NEXT PAGE.

You look down, trying to see where the horrible sound came from. Both of the support struts holding the Ferris wheel in place have burst into splinters!

A shudder runs through the wheel. Then it drops, thudding onto the ground. Slowly, it begins to roll!

"We're going to die!" Rick screams.

Laura is completely quiet. Her hands grip the safety bar so tightly that her knuckles are turning white. Desperately, you look around, trying to figure out something to do, anything that will keep you alive.

The only idea that comes to you seems crazy, but it's better than nothing.

"Maybe we can jump!" you shout. "Wait until the basket is close to the ground and hop off before it goes back up. Jump from the back, though. So the wheel doesn't crush us!"

Rick looks at you with wide eyes. "No way! Are you insane?!"

GO ON TO THE NEXT PAGE.

Rick won't budge, and Laura seems completely paralyzed by fear.

WILL YOU . . .

. . . try jumping by yourself?
TURN TO PAGE 102.

. . . try to haul Laura along with you?
TURN TO PAGE 11.

. . . ride it out?
TURN TO PAGE 76.

"Three!"

You thump onto the tracks, but . . . something is weird. You didn't hit very hard. The tracks should be on a slope, but they're not.

Rick looks confused too. "What in the—?"

You're not high up on the coaster. You're still in the station!

"Where's Laura?"

Rick shakes his head and shrugs.

Then you both see a pale hand slung over the last car. Inside, you find Laura slumped on the seat, her face twisted up with terror.

"It . . . it looks like she was scared to death!" you say.

The Barker is standing on the platform, but he's not the Barker anymore. He has turned back into the wrinkled old man. "All that effort and only one down?" He scowls. "Barely worth it!"

A wave of anger washes over you. "I'll fix that!" you hear yourself scream.

Suddenly fearful, the little man takes off running.

GO ON TO THE NEXT PAGE.

Rick grabs your arm. He's angry too but thinks you should get out before what happened to Laura happens to you.

WILL YOU . . .

. . . chase down the old guy and punish him for killing Laura?
TURN TO PAGE 74.

. . . get away while you can?
TURN TO PAGE 58.

You tell the Barker you'll just wait for your friends.

"Oh, come now," he replies. "Don't be a spoilsport. Hop on up there."

When you tell him "no thanks," he gives you a nasty glare.

Laura climbs up on the silver gray horse. Rick picks a white one.

"Come on!" Laura calls over to you. "It'll be fun."

"Probably more for me than for you, young lady," the Barker says.

Suddenly you know something is wrong. The carousel horses change. They get larger and more monstrous. Black water drips from their coats. Their eyes are wild.

"Hey!" shouts Rick. "What's going on?"

The horses leap down from the carousel and gallop furiously toward the big pond.

"Jump!" you scream. "Jump!"

But Rick and Laura cling to the horses as if they're stuck in place.

GO ON TO THE NEXT PAGE.

You run to the water's edge as the horses plunge beneath the water's surface.

WILL YOU . . .

. . . get out of there, before something happens to you too?

TURN TO PAGE 85.

. . . dive into the lake to help your friends?

TURN TO PAGE 49.

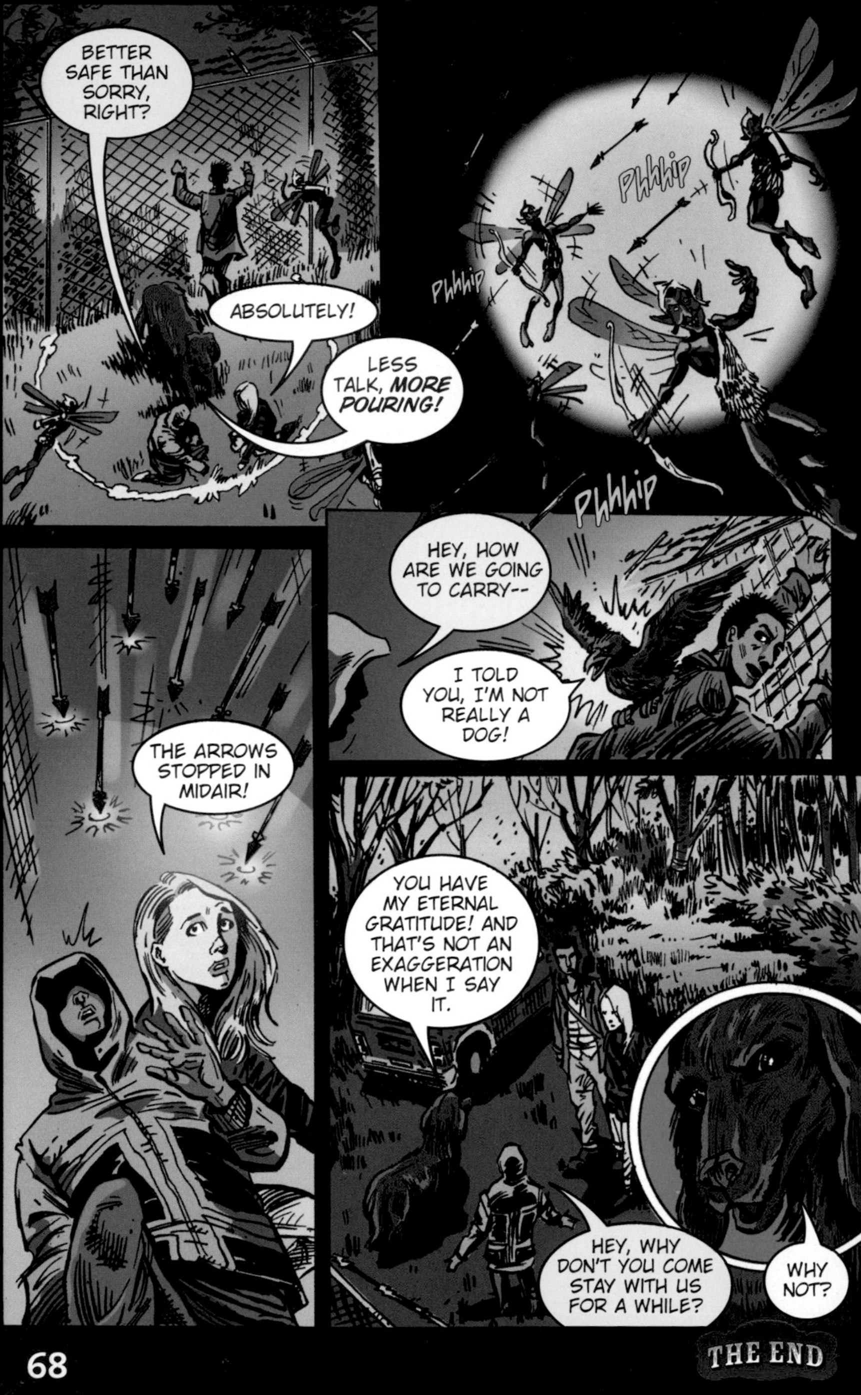

BETTER SAFE THAN SORRY, RIGHT?
ABSOLUTELY!
LESS TALK, **MORE POURING!**
Phhhip
Phhhip
Phhhip
HEY, HOW ARE WE GOING TO CARRY--
I TOLD YOU, I'M NOT REALLY A DOG!
THE ARROWS STOPPED IN MIDAIR!
YOU HAVE MY ETERNAL GRATITUDE! AND THAT'S NOT AN EXAGGERATION WHEN I SAY IT.
HEY, WHY DON'T YOU COME STAY WITH US FOR A WHILE?
WHY NOT?
THE END

Figuring there's nothing you can do to help Rick, you grab Laura by the arm and try to drag her away.

"We've got to go!" you whisper.

After a second's pause, she comes with you. You start to run.

Behind you, the Far Darrig starts to yell. "Stop 'em! Don't let 'em get away!"

Then you hear Rick's terrified scream. He's coming up behind you fast!

You glance back to see Rick hurtling toward you, thrown by the monstrously strong creature that grabbed him. You try to warn Laura, but Rick smashes into you both.

The air rushes out of your lungs as you hit the ground. Something in your chest cracks, and you struggle to breathe your final breaths.

THE END

You edge toward one of the courtyard's exits. "She looks kind of weird. Let's just keep moving."

Laura follows after you, but Rick hesitates.

"Come on! Look at her," he says. "She can't hurt us."

"You don't know that," Laura says.

Rick shrugs and walks over to the woman. "Sorry about my friends," he says. "They're just scared of all the weirdness going on."

"Well they should be," the woman answers. She smiles widely. Even across the courtyard you can tell her crooked teeth are the blue-green color of old copper. "Guess you'll have to be company enough for Jenny Greenteeth!"

Her grin reveals more teeth than any mouth should hold. Clawlike nails sprout from her fingertips. Before you can blink, she's locked her teeth and claws into your friend!

Laura screams Rick's name, but you drag her toward one of the courtyard exits. You know there's nothing you can do for him.

GO TO PAGE 86.

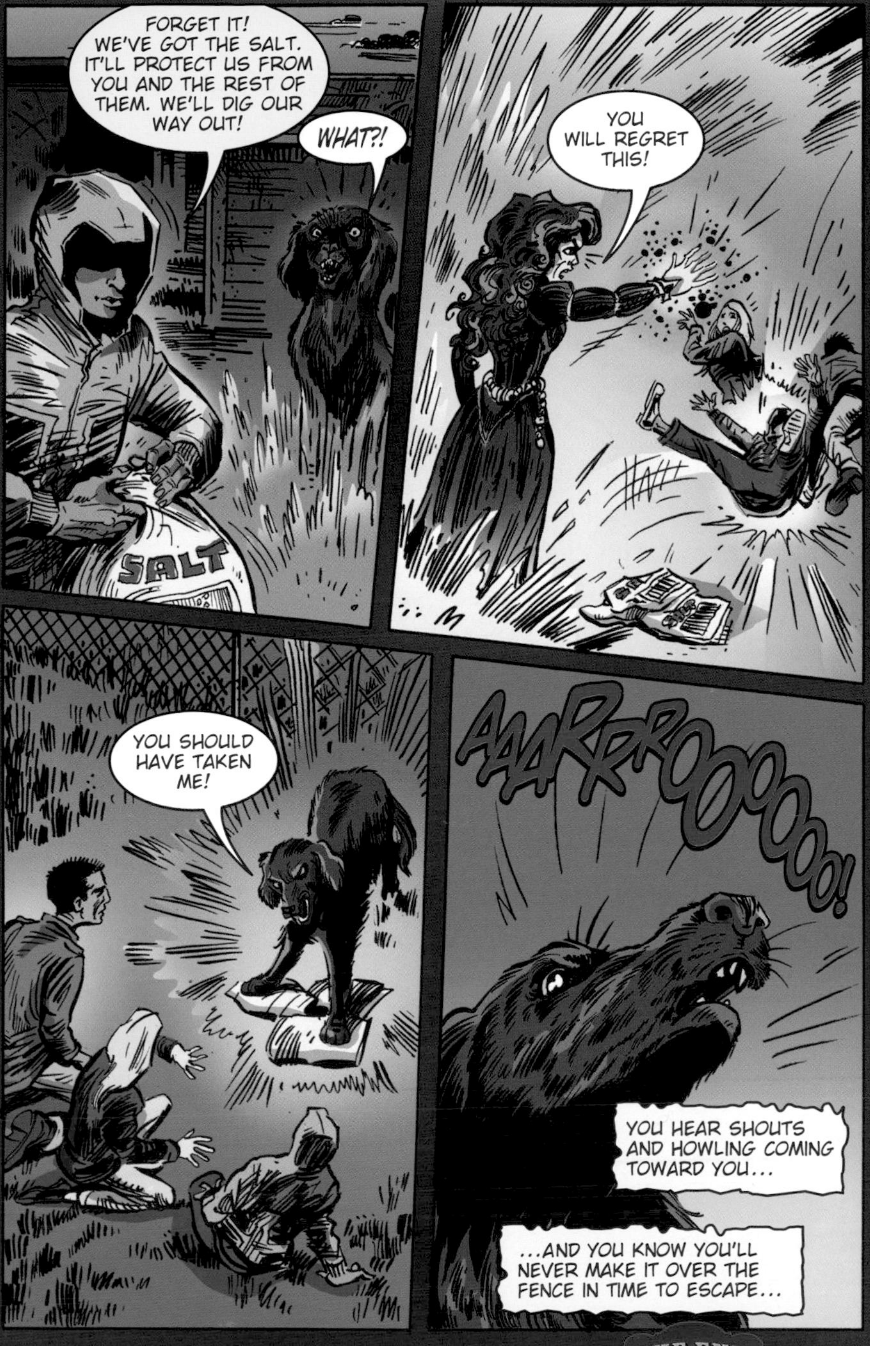
FORGET IT! WE'VE GOT THE SALT. IT'LL PROTECT US FROM YOU AND THE REST OF THEM. WE'LL DIG OUR WAY OUT!
WHAT?!
SALT
YOU WILL REGRET THIS!
YOU SHOULD HAVE TAKEN ME!
AAARRROOOOOOO!
YOU HEAR SHOUTS AND HOWLING COMING TOWARD YOU...
...AND YOU KNOW YOU'LL NEVER MAKE IT OVER THE FENCE IN TIME TO ESCAPE...

THE END

Since Rick and Laura both seem to want to go to the Tunnel of Love, you reluctantly agree.

"Hope it's at least a scary one," you mutter. "Not all cupids and hearts."

"Something for everyone!" the Barker laughs. He helps you into the boats and wishes you bon voyage.

This Tunnel of Love *isn't* one of the scary ones. It's all hearts and flowers and rainbows. Plus, Rick and Laura are whispering and laughing quietly to each other. You feel left out.

Suddenly Laura points at something ahead. "Oooooo, look at the cupid!"

You squint at the thing flying toward you. It's not like any cupid you've ever seen. It's not chubby, for starters. Plus, its wings are all wrong. More like insect wings than angel wings. The arrow it has drawn in its bow looks pretty dangerous!

It fires its bow, and Rick slumps over.

GO ON TO THE NEXT PAGE.

YOU REALIZE RICK IS COMPLETELY PARALYZED. NUMB. CAN'T FEEL A THING. *JUST LIKE YOU.*

YOU DON'T EVEN FEEL THE FIRST BITE THE ARCHER TAKES OUT OF YOU. OR ANY OF THE REST...

THE END

You leap to the platform and start chasing the little red man. After a second, Rick follows.

For a stumpy-legged guy, the red man is fast. You can't seem to catch him. Even Rick, with his longer legs, is having trouble getting closer.

As the red man races through the park, you manage to keep him in sight. He cuts through empty buildings and scrambles over rides, but you and Rick aren't going to give up.

Finally, he scrambles through a narrow gap between two midway booths. It's a tight squeeze and you pick up some splinters, but you and Rick keep after him.

As you push your way out from between the buildings, you see . . .

GO ON TO THE NEXT PAGE.

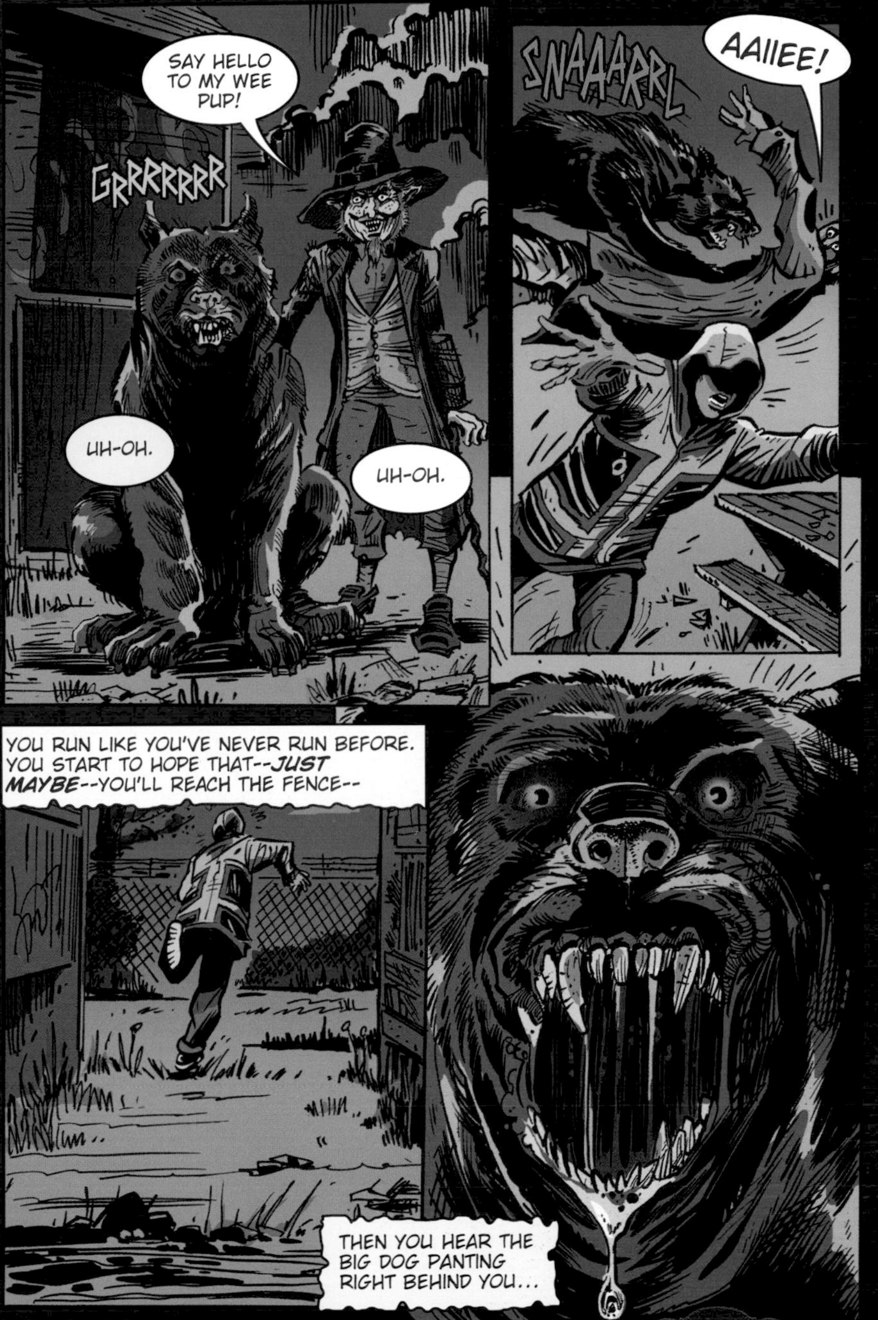
SAY HELLO TO MY WEE PUP!
GRRRRRR
UH-OH.
UH-OH.
SNAAARRL
AAIIEE!
YOU RUN LIKE YOU'VE NEVER RUN BEFORE. YOU START TO HOPE THAT--*JUST MAYBE*--YOU'LL REACH THE FENCE--
THEN YOU HEAR THE BIG DOG PANTING RIGHT BEHIND YOU...
THE END

Maybe Rick is right. If you just ride it out, there's a chance the Ferris wheel will stop.

You fight to hold on as the wheel picks up speed instead. It crashes through the fence and the trees beyond. Amazingly, the wheel just keeps rolling right into the woods.

"Maybe the trees will slow us down!" Rick sobs. "Maybe they'll hold the wheel up when it stops."

"Maybe," you whisper, just as the wheel hits a big pine tree and spins like a quarter on a tabletop. You've got a great view, because you're in the highest basket.

Finally, the Ferris wheel topples sideways. You and Rick scream all the way down.

THE END

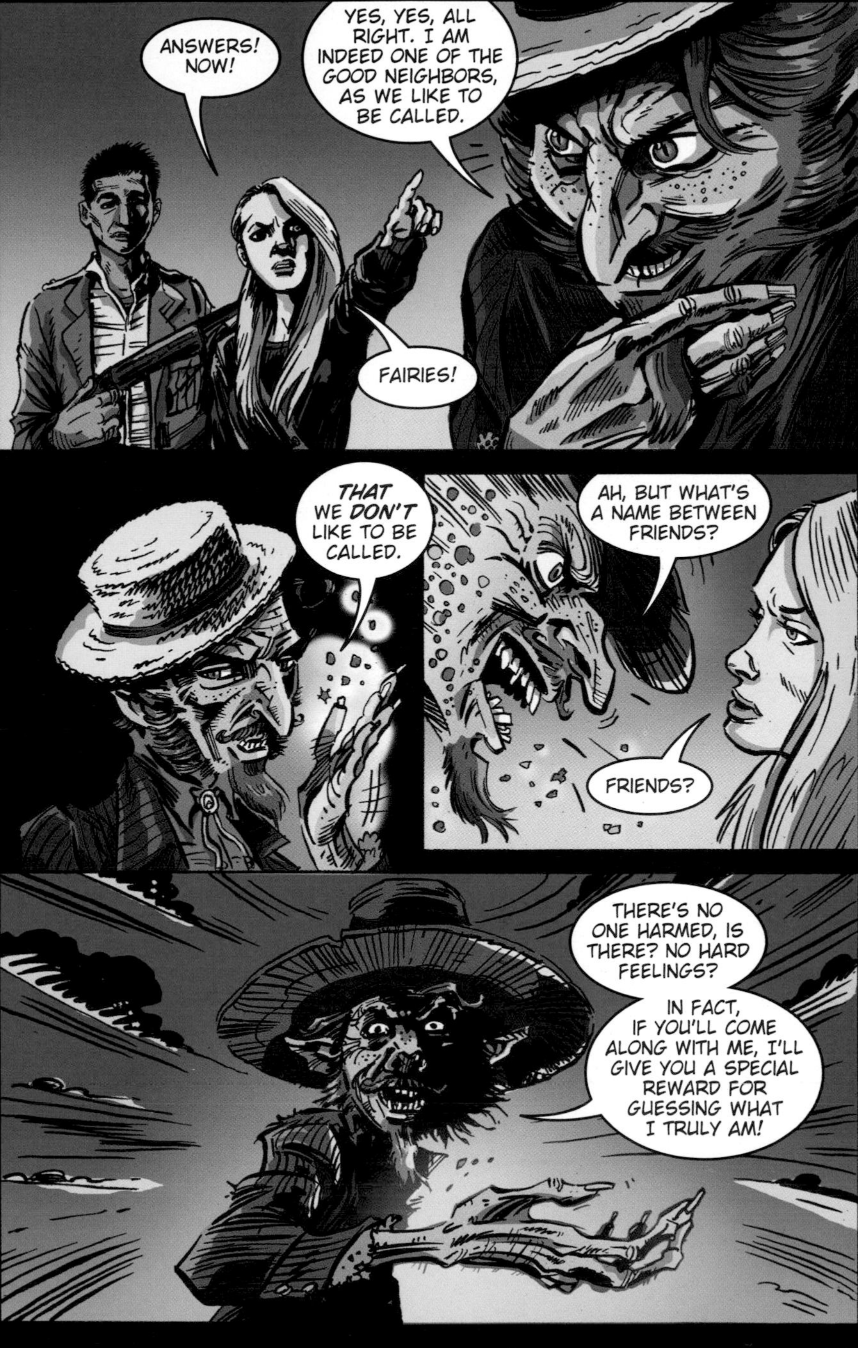
ANSWERS! NOW!
YES, YES, ALL RIGHT. I AM INDEED ONE OF THE GOOD NEIGHBORS, AS WE LIKE TO BE CALLED.
FAIRIES!
THAT WE DON'T LIKE TO BE CALLED.
AH, BUT WHAT'S A NAME BETWEEN FRIENDS?
FRIENDS?
THERE'S NO ONE HARMED, IS THERE? NO HARD FEELINGS?
IN FACT, IF YOU'LL COME ALONG WITH ME, I'LL GIVE YOU A SPECIAL REWARD FOR GUESSING WHAT I TRULY AM!

GO ON TO THE NEXT PAGE.

It'd be nice to get something for your troubles.

WILL YOU . . .

. . . leave the amusement park before he tries another prank?
TURN TO PAGE 33.

. . . go and get the reward he's promising?
TURN TO PAGE 80.

"These aren't going to do much good!" you yell, throwing your BB rifle to the ground. Rick does the same. You both start running.

The elephant has picked up Laura with its trunk, but you can't think of anything you can do about it. You keep running.

Within a few strides, Rick's long legs carry him past you. You wish you could run like that.

Then something even faster blurs by you. It's the cheetah!

Within seconds, it catches up with Rick. Snarling, it leaps on his back, knocking him to the ground.

Horrified, you stop dead in your tracks. Then you feel the ground tremble.

You turn, just in time for the water buffalo to run you down.

THE END

The three of you exchange glances.

"Why not?" you say. "He owes us something for scaring us half to death!"

Rick grins. "Plus, we've got the BB guns in case of trouble."

Laura seems a little less sure but says OK.

The little red man brings you to the weathered remains of the Haunted Castle, Summerland's chamber of horrors. It's held up pretty well, though there are places where the paint has worn away and you can tell its massive stones are just plaster.

The gates are open, and the portcullis is up. Still, it looks less than inviting.

"Come along," the red man says cheerily. "Your reward awaits!"

He leads you down dark corridors strewn with spiderwebs. You're not sure if the webs are real or fake.

 "Just up ahead!" the red man calls back.

Soon he points at a shadowy doorway. "Right in here," he says loudly. "Nothing to fear. I'll go in first!"

GO ON TO THE NEXT PAGE.

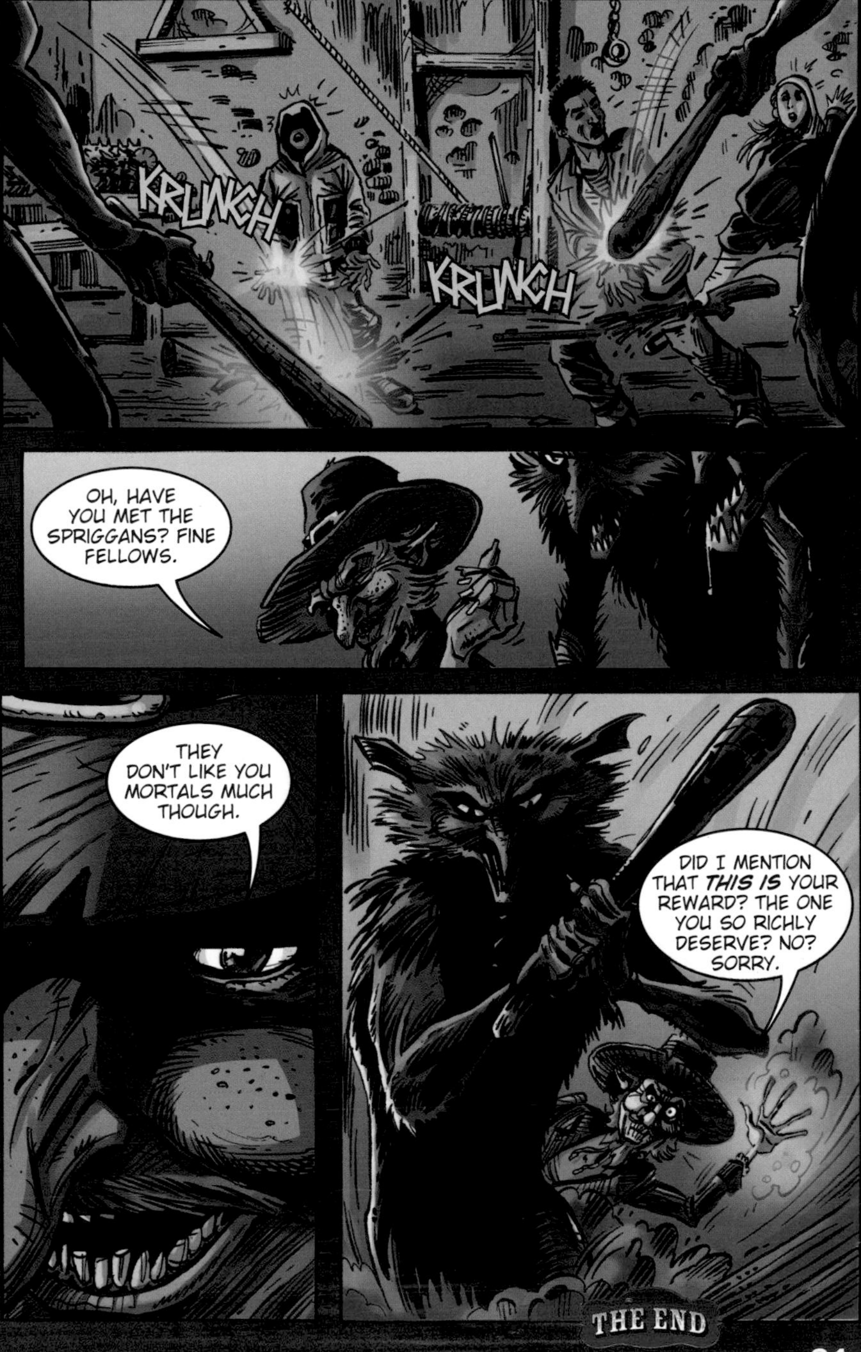
KRUNCH
KRUNCH
OH, HAVE YOU MET THE SPRIGGANS? FINE FELLOWS.
THEY DON'T LIKE YOU MORTALS MUCH THOUGH.
DID I MENTION THAT *THIS IS* YOUR REWARD? THE ONE YOU SO RICHLY DESERVE? NO? SORRY.
THE END

Almost without thinking, you jump forward and poke the corkscrew of your multi-tool into the arm of the creature holding Rick!

Bellowing with pain, the spriggan lets go and stumbles back. It holds its wounded arm out in front of it, as if trying to get the wound as far away from its body as possible. The arm is starting to smoke!

The rest of the creatures back away as their injured comrade falls to his knees, whimpering. The wound bubbles and blackens, streaming more and more smoke. The burning spreads, faster and faster, all over its skin.

Taking advantage of their distraction, you drag Rick away and hiss for Laura to follow you.

GO ON TO THE NEXT PAGE.

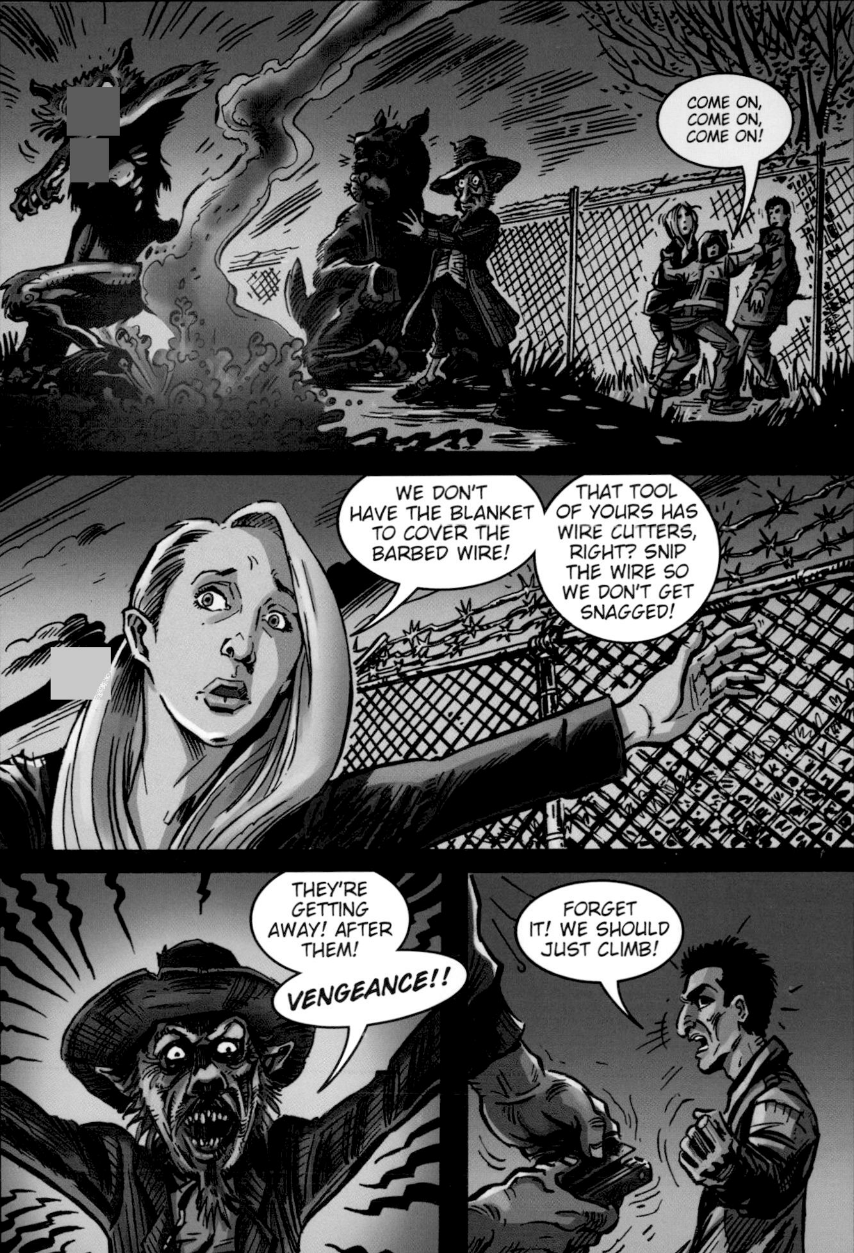

COME ON, COME ON, COME ON!
WE DON'T HAVE THE BLANKET TO COVER THE BARBED WIRE!
THAT TOOL OF YOURS HAS WIRE CUTTERS, RIGHT? SNIP THE WIRE SO WE DON'T GET SNAGGED!
THEY'RE GETTING AWAY! AFTER THEM!
VENGEANCE!!
FORGET IT! WE SHOULD JUST CLIMB!

They're coming! You might not have time to get rid of the barbed wire.

WILL YOU . . .

. . . risk getting cut or snagged by the wire?
TURN TO PAGE 93.

. . . cut the barbed wire?
TURN TO PAGE 57.

There's no way you can rescue them. They're gone. The Barker stands nearby, laughing.

"Coward!" he sneers. "Aren't you even going to try and save your friends?"

You want to show him you're not a coward. But if he can conjure monsters like those horses, there's no telling what else he can do. Ashamed, you turn and run for the fence.

When you reach it, you make a running jump and grab the top bar, just below the barbed wire. Ignoring the sharp barbs, you haul yourself over and drop to the ground.

Looking back through the fence, you see nothing more than the abandoned amusement park you saw when you arrived a few hours ago. There's no sign of the Barker. No sign of your lost friends.

It's like nothing ever happened, except that they're gone.

THE END

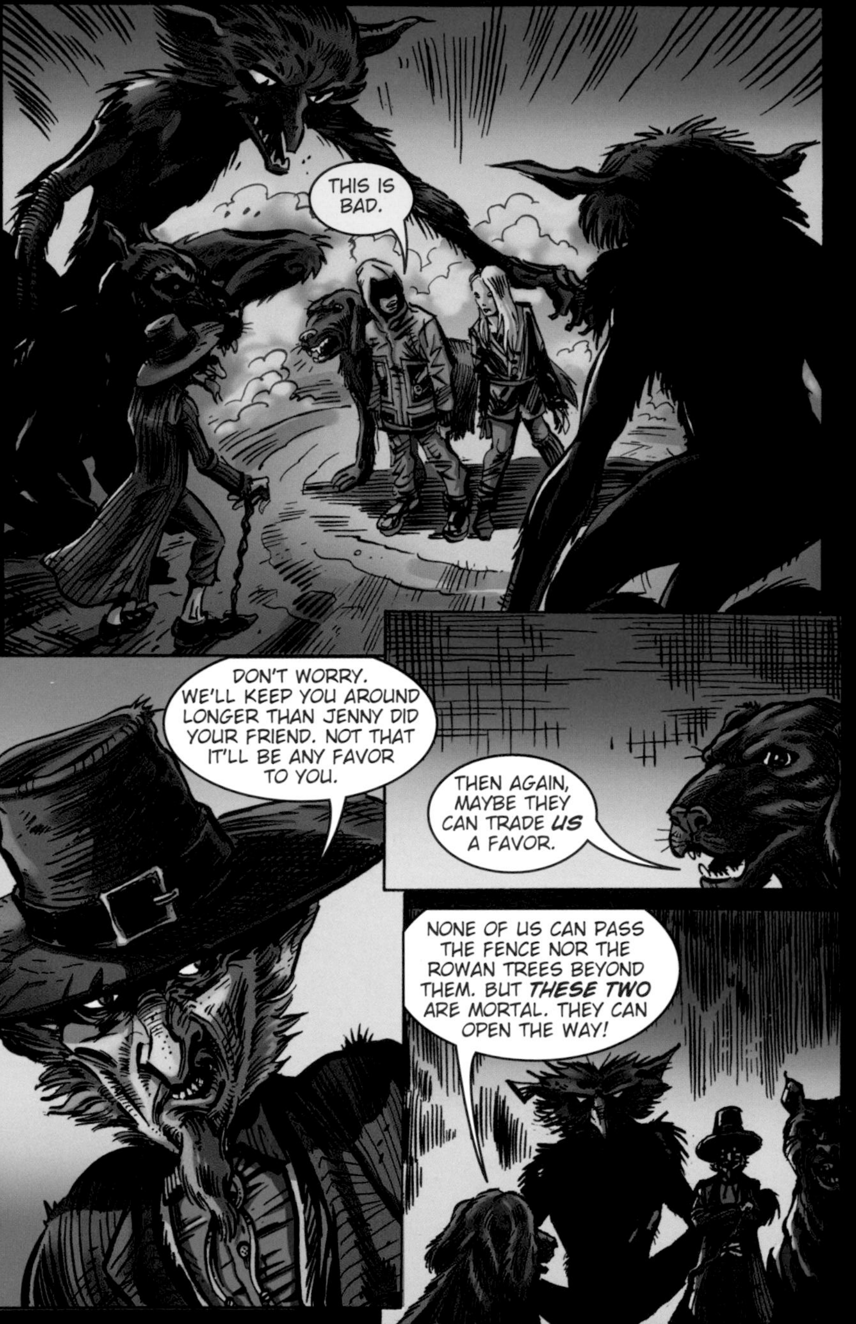
THIS IS BAD.
DON'T WORRY. WE'LL KEEP YOU AROUND LONGER THAN JENNY DID YOUR FRIEND. NOT THAT IT'LL BE ANY FAVOR TO YOU.
THEN AGAIN, MAYBE THEY CAN TRADE *US* A FAVOR.
NONE OF US CAN PASS THE FENCE NOR THE ROWAN TREES BEYOND THEM. BUT *THESE TWO* ARE MORTAL. THEY CAN OPEN THE WAY!

GO ON TO THE NEXT PAGE.

The little red man howls at the dog. "We can't trust 'em! What if they cut the fence but leave the iron bar across the road?"

Still, the other creatures begin to mutter among themselves.

"If you'll free us from this place, we'll swear to let you leave unharmed," says the dog. "But know that an oath to our kind is binding. Betray us and there will be . . . consequences."

After what happened to Rick, you and Laura immediately agree. You've got a multi-tool in your pocket with wire cutters. It takes awhile, but you're able to cut open the fence. Next, you cover the iron bar across the road with dirt.

The red dog waits with you as the other creatures march past, disappearing into the woods. The red man leaves last, glaring at you as he goes.

The dog barks a happy laugh. "It's good to be free!"

Suddenly it changes into a big, red horse! "Can I offer you a ride?"

The red horse seems grateful, but can you trust it
after what the thing from the well did to Rick?

WILL YOU . . .

. . . take the ride?
TURN TO PAGE 101.

. . . go back for the car?
TURN TO PAGE 38.

"If we're going to trust . . . um . . . Setter," you say, "we might as well trust all the way. Questions can wait."

Rick grumbles but agrees.

The dog cautiously leads you around buildings and rides until you reach the Snack Shack. Then you all slip inside.

"Okay," you say, "How about some answers?"

The dog points its nose toward a shelf. "Drag down those bags of salt while I explain."

Rick shrugs and reaches for a bag.

"As to what I am," Setter says, "have you ever heard tell of a pooka?"

Laura stares at Setter. "Pooka? That's a kind of fai—"

A low growl interrupts her.

You think for a second. "Um, I think I read that they don't like that name."

Laura blushes. "Right. Sorry. Go on."

"When the people who named this region first arrived from Ireland," says Setter, "they brought their beliefs with them. That meant my folk came along too."

GO ON TO THE NEXT PAGE.

"THOUGH THE VARIETY OF MY FOLK IS ENDLESS, THERE ARE TWO MAIN SORTS. THERE ARE THE COURTLY TYPES, TALL, FAIR, AND PROUD..."

"...AND THOSE WHO ARE MORE MISCHIEVOUS BY NATURE, LIKE ME. SOME OF US DELIGHT IN PLAYING PRANKS ON YOU MORTALS. OTHERS LOVE TO DO YOU HARM."

"THE FAR DARRIG, THAT WRINKLED RUNT THAT HUNTS YOU, IS ONE OF THOSE."

"HE WAS DRAWN HERE BY THE FEAR YOU INFLICT ON YOURSELVES IN SO-CALLED AMUSEMENT PARKS. SO WERE OTHERS."

"AT FIRST WE JUST INDULGED IN SIMPLE TRICKS AND SMALL FRIGHTS. THEN THE FAR DARRIG SCARED A MAN TO DEATH. IT SO PLEASED HIM THAT HE COULD NOT STOP."

GO ON TO THE NEXT PAGE.

Setter sighs heavily. "A wise woman from the old country realized what was happening and told the owner. Together, they made a plan. The park closed for renovations. The fence went up. To keep people out, we thought. At first, it had a gate. None of us worried. Then they started planting rowan trees, and we understood what was really happening."

Rick looks puzzled. "Rowan? With the red berries?"

Setter nods. "They protect against my kind."

Laura holds up a bag. "Like salt, right? That's why you brought us here!"

"And iron!" you say. "Is that why there's a rail sunk into the road?"

"Just so," says Setter. "When the trees and rail were in place, we were ringed 'round twice. The owner even replaced the gate with plain fence for good measure."

Setter's ears twitch up. "Do you hear? The tread of heavy feet? The Far Darrig has called out the spriggans. Vicious sorts. We should go. Quietly."

Rick thinks that you should make a break for the
fence. Laura wants to hole up where you are.
Setter says you must go. Now.

WILL YOU . . .

. . . sneak away?
TURN TO PAGE 50.

. . . make a run for the fence?
TURN TO PAGE 42.

. . . make a stand at the Snack Shack?
TURN TO PAGE 97.

You stick the multi-tool back into your pocket. "Just climb!" you yell.

Rick is already halfway up the fence as you and Laura start to climb. Getting only a few cuts, he clears the barbed wire and drops to the ground. You follow a second later. You panic momentarily as the bottom of your pant leg snags, but it tears free as you drop.

You hear another ripping sound as Laura tumbles to the ground. Glancing up, you see the sleeve of her coat fluttering in the wind.

Laura gives you an embarrassed grin as she checks out her missing sleeve. "Guess I'm going to need a new coat."

You start to laugh, but then you catch a glimpse of the angry eyes of the creatures on the other side of the fence.

"I know they can't climb the metal fence." You gulp. "But let's get out of here anyway!"

Your friends agree.

THE END

"It's probably a trap!" you say, turning to run. Your friends are right behind you.

The red dog calls out, "Wait! Come back!" Suddenly the other dog, the drooling black hellhound, scrambles around the corner a couple of buildings ahead of you.

Sprinting across the midway, you squeeze between the ring toss stand and a skee-ball booth.

As your friends follow, you tell them, "No way that monster can fit through here!" The frustrated howling you hear behind you says that you're right.

At the other end, you come out into a weed-filled courtyard. At the center, you see a wishing well.

GO ON TO THE NEXT PAGE.

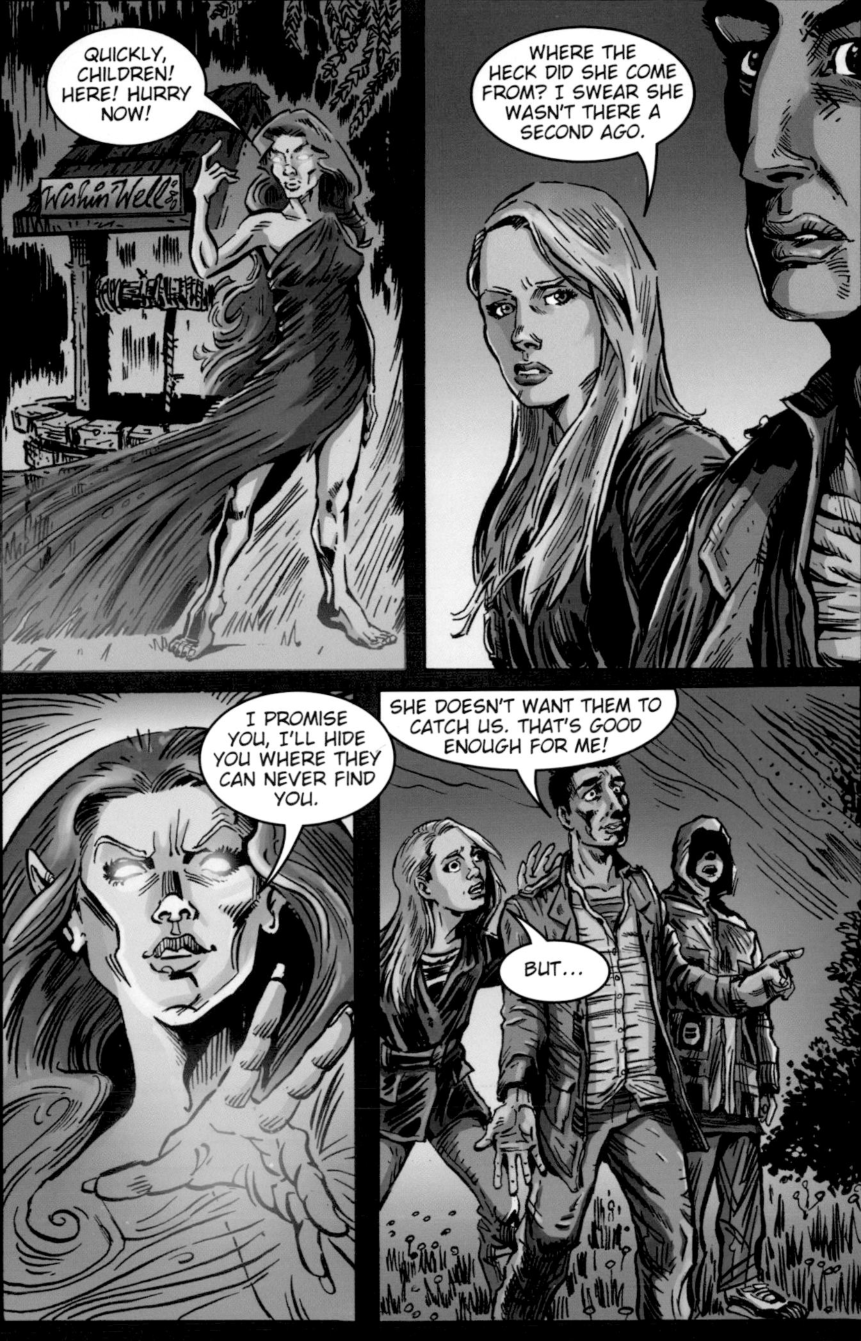
QUICKLY, CHILDREN! HERE! HURRY NOW!
Wishin' Well
WHERE THE HECK DID SHE COME FROM? I SWEAR SHE WASN'T THERE A SECOND AGO.
I PROMISE YOU, I'LL HIDE YOU WHERE THEY CAN NEVER FIND YOU.
SHE DOESN'T WANT THEM TO CATCH US. THAT'S GOOD ENOUGH FOR ME!
BUT...

GO ON TO THE NEXT PAGE.

The lady seems more normal than anyone else you've seen inside the park.

WILL YOU . . .

. . . avoid her?
TURN TO PAGE 70.

. . . accept her offer?
TURN TO PAGE 109.

"Laura's right!" you say. "If we protect ourselves with a circle of salt, they can't hurt us."

The three of you tear open your bags of salt and begin to make a big circle. Setter shakes her head sadly. Then she bolts out the back door.

It isn't long before the Far Darrig comes in through the front door. He gives the ring of salt a close look.

"Well now," he says, "I won't be getting at you, will I?"

Laura smirks. "No. You won't!"

"Then again," he says, "neither will you be going anywhere soon."

With a nasty grin, he knocks a big jug of cooking oil from a nearby shelf. The top pops off as it hits the ground. The stuff starts pouring out over the floor.

"I'll just leave you in safety," he says. He snaps his fingers and a spark flies from them to the oily floor.

The flames leap up around you. As he leaves, he calls back, "My warmest regards!"

THE END

"We have to do the coaster first," you insist. "It's the best part of any amusement park! The crowning glory!"

Laura frowns. "Then shouldn't we save the best for last?"

You laugh. "Life's too short to save the best for last!"

Laura looks over to Rick. He shrugs. "Kind of has a point."

Rolling her eyes, Laura agrees.

You pump your fists in the air. "Yes!"

The Barker gives you all a sly smile and bows just a little, pointing toward the roller coaster. "The roller coaster it is. Your wish is my command."

GO ON TO THE NEXT PAGE.

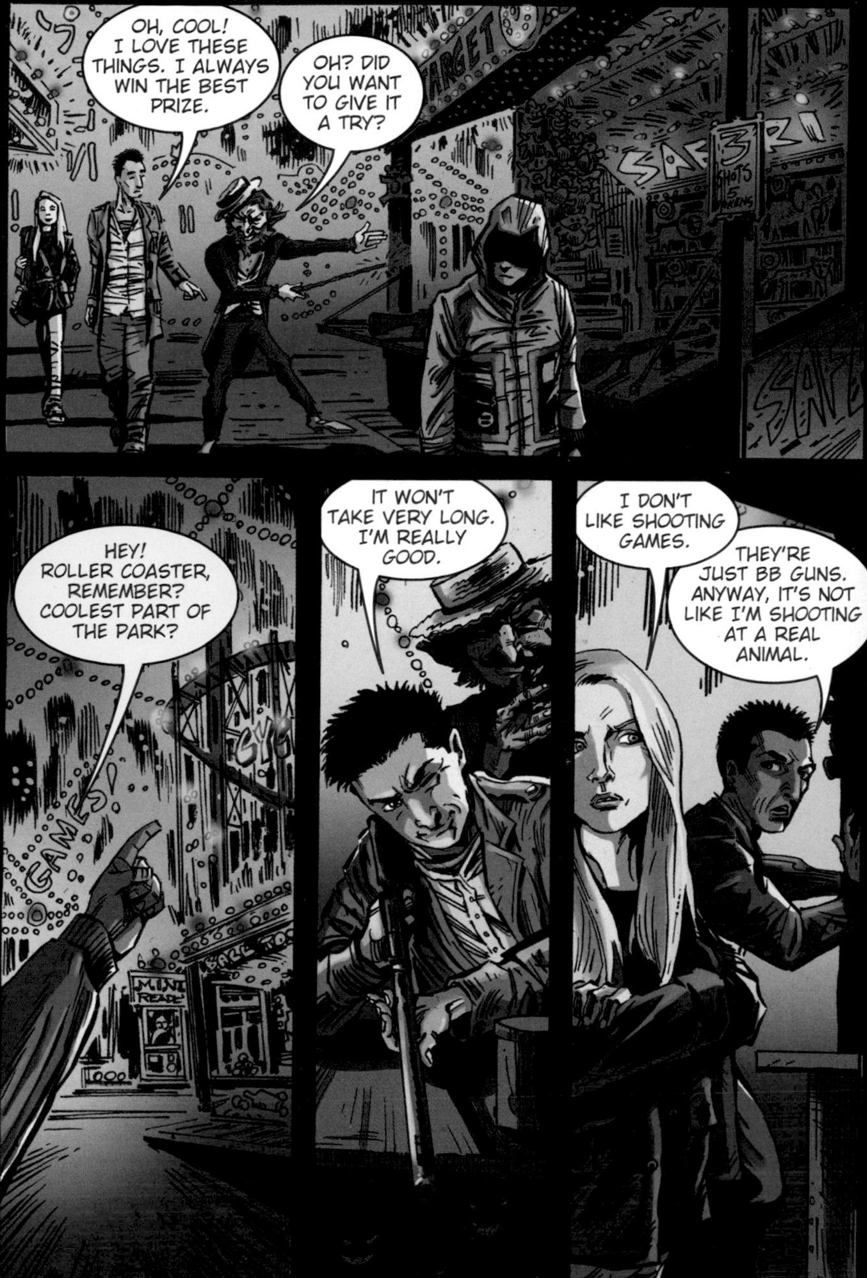
OH, COOL! I LOVE THESE THINGS. I ALWAYS WIN THE BEST PRIZE.
OH? DID YOU WANT TO GIVE IT A TRY?
HEY! ROLLER COASTER, REMEMBER? COOLEST PART OF THE PARK?
IT WON'T TAKE VERY LONG. I'M REALLY GOOD.
I DON'T LIKE SHOOTING GAMES.
THEY'RE JUST BB GUNS. ANYWAY, IT'S NOT LIKE I'M SHOOTING AT A REAL ANIMAL.

GO ON TO THE NEXT PAGE.

Laura seems pretty upset.

WILL YOU . . .

. . . make Rick stick to the plan and
do the roller coaster first?
TURN TO PAGE 54.

. . . let Rick have this one?
TURN TO PAGE 106.

Laura wants to get the car, but you remember that Rick had the keys.

You're both a little nervous as you climb onto the red horse's bare back.

"Don't worry," it reassures you as the two of you climb on, "I won't let you fall."

Then it leaps forward and bursts into a gallop.

"Just give me directions as we go," it says.

Glancing back, you can't help sighing sadly. "Poor Rick."

The horse gives a quick bob of its head. "It's a shame about your friend. If you'd listened to me earlier, he might still be with us and there would be less mischief loosed upon the world."

The horse passes under the big Summerland sign as the sky starts to lighten, then turns at your direction and races down the road. The wind rushes over your faces, drying the tears that you and Laura shed.

THE END

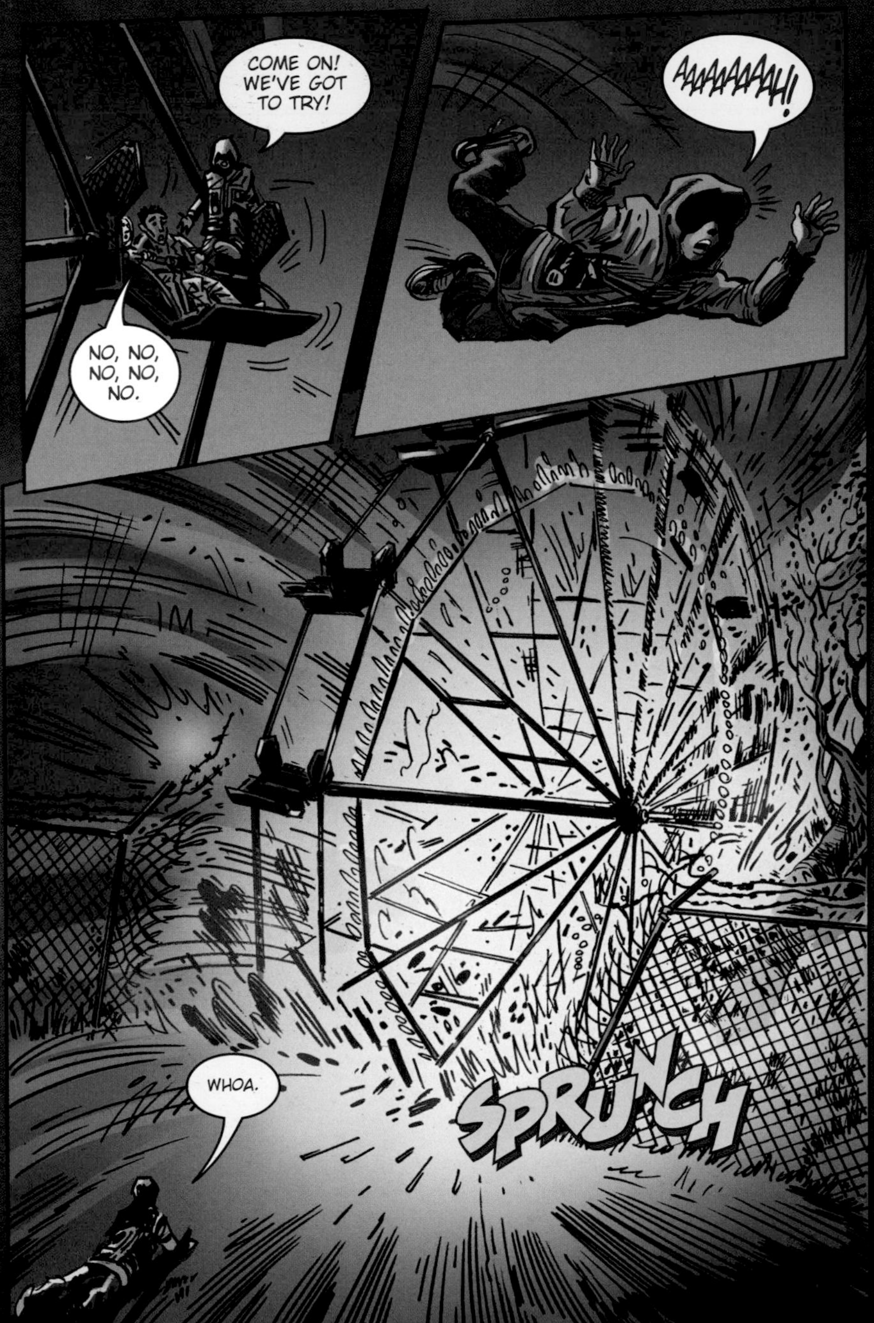
COME ON! WE'VE GOT TO TRY!
NO, NO, NO, NO, NO.
AAAAAAAAAH!
WHOA.
SPRUNCH

GO ON TO THE NEXT PAGE.

You jump to your feet and chase after the wheel, hoping you'll be able to help your friends when it stops.

The wheel doesn't get far before it gets tangled in the trees beyond the fence. It wobbles . . . tips . . . then topples sideways.

You hear screaming as it falls, drowned out by the tremendous crash of the wheel smashing into the ground.

You fall to your knees, devastated by what's happened to your friends.

Then a gravelly voice snarls, "Well, well. Looks like one of you managed to survive."

GO ON TO THE NEXT PAGE.

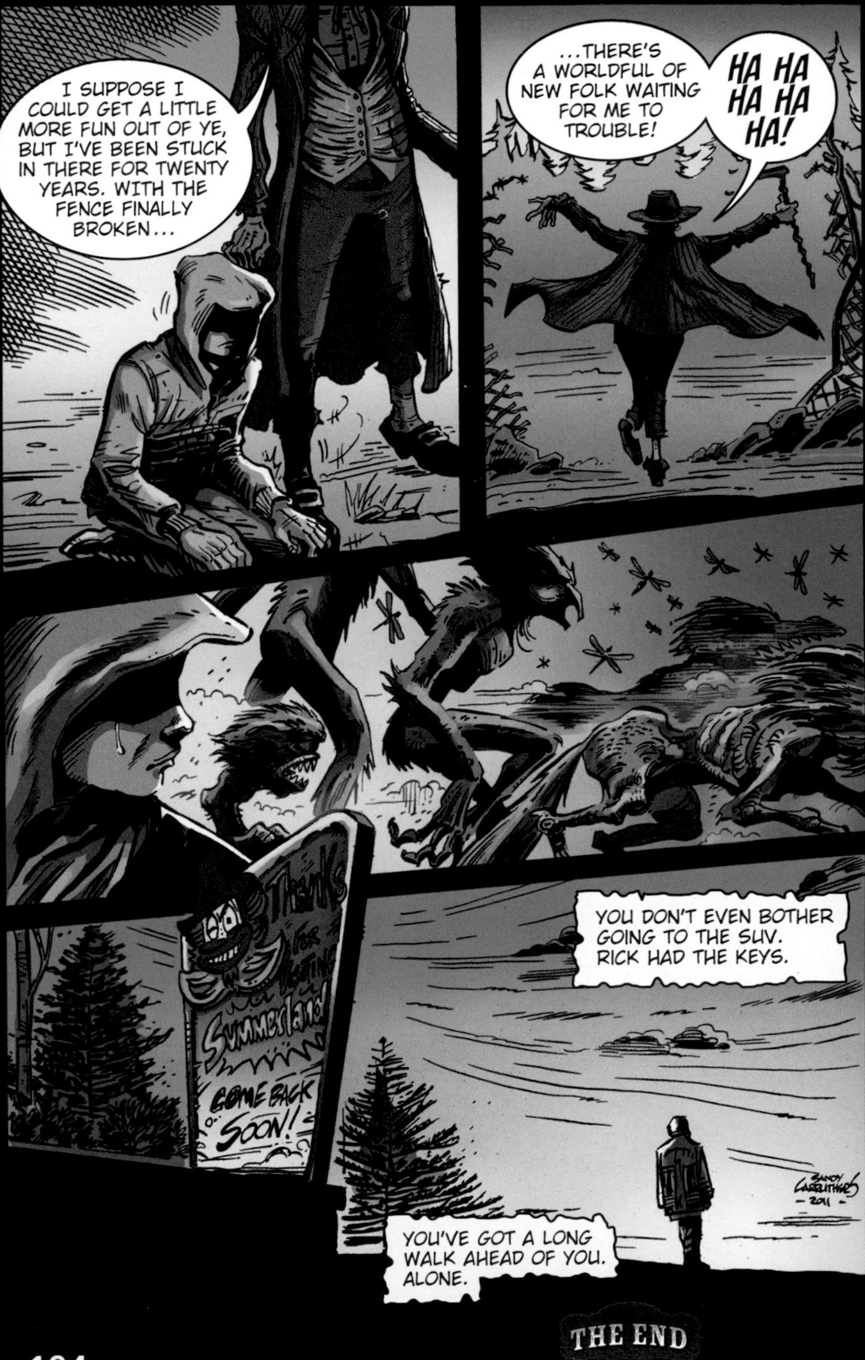

I SUPPOSE I COULD GET A LITTLE MORE FUN OUT OF YE, BUT I'VE BEEN STUCK IN THERE FOR TWENTY YEARS. WITH THE FENCE FINALLY BROKEN...
...THERE'S A WORLDFUL OF NEW FOLK WAITING FOR ME TO TROUBLE!
HA HA HA HA HA!
Thanks for Visiting Summerland
COME BACK SOON!
YOU DON'T EVEN BOTHER GOING TO THE SUV. RICK HAD THE KEYS.
YOU'VE GOT A LONG WALK AHEAD OF YOU. ALONE.
THE END

Maybe Rick's right. Maybe jumping at the last second is your best chance.

You and Rick slide out from under the safety bar and stand on the seat. The speed of the roller coaster whips your hair around. You can barely hear a thing.

You notice that Laura is still in her seat. You reach out your hand and yell, "Come on!" She shakes her head, closes her eyes, and clutches the safety bar tighter.

You're almost at the gap in the tracks. It's too late to help her. You give Rick a quick glance. He tries to smile but can't. He says something that you can't quite hear. You think it was "good luck!"

Just before the car goes off the tracks, you both jump!

As you fall, all you can hear is the sound of rushing wind. When you see Rick collide with the ground, you know you've made a terrible mistake.

THE END

"Okay," you say. "Let's give it a try."

You and Rick pick up the BB guns. They're already loaded. Laura has walked a few yards away, standing with her back to you and her arms crossed.

"So who goes first?" you ask.

"Go ahead." He grins.

You take aim, and the targets start flipping up at random. It's harder than you expected, but you hit quite a few before they all pop down again.

"My turn," says Rick.

Pling! Pling! Pling! He doesn't miss a single one.

"Told you I was good," he says. Then he turns and calls out to Laura. "You sure you don't want to take a turn?"

Laura turns toward you and starts to say something but stops. Her eyes go wide. Behind you, a loud trumpeting sound echoes out of the shooting gallery.

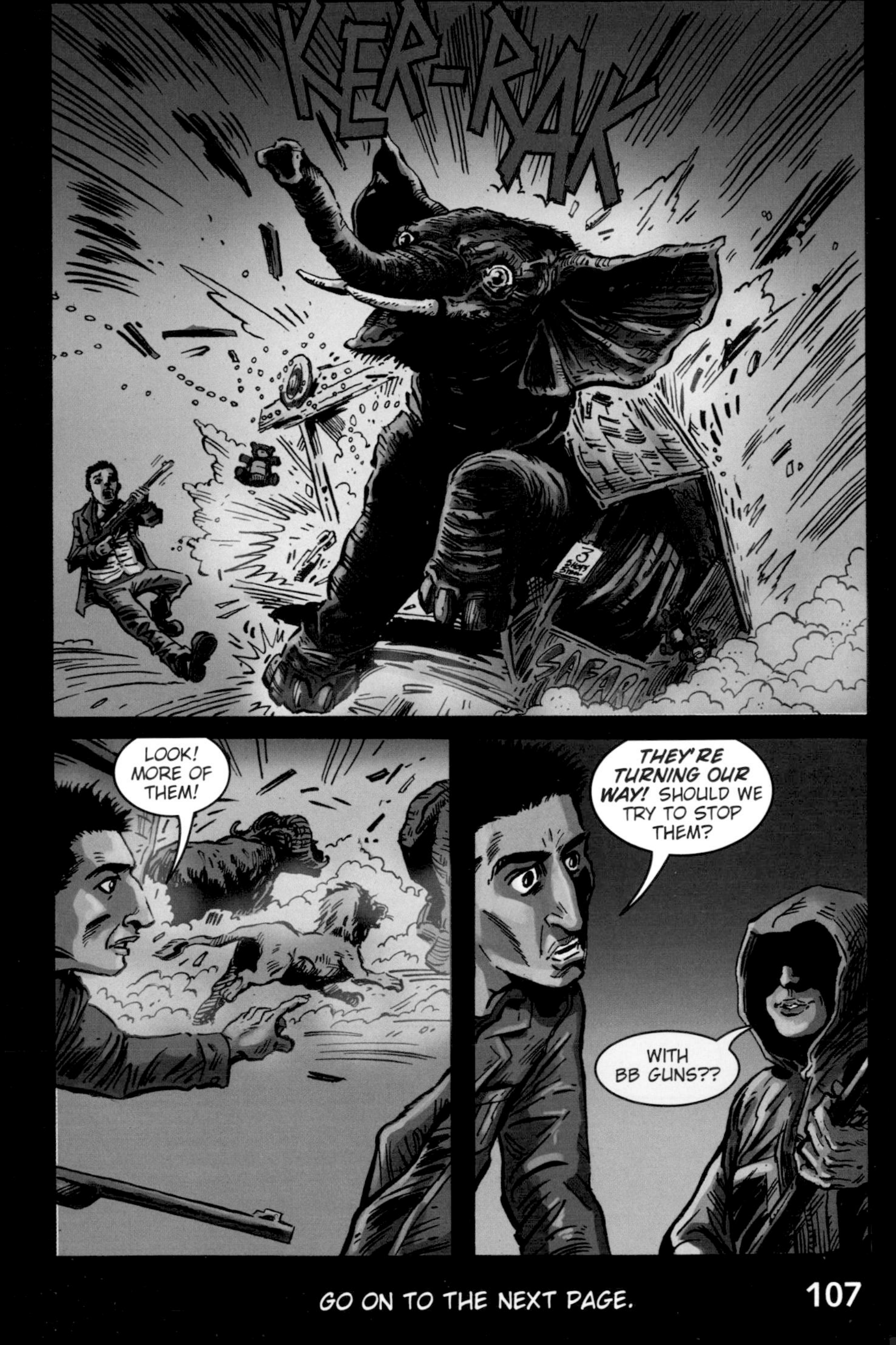
KER-RAK
SAFARI
LOOK! MORE OF THEM!
THEY'RE TURNING OUR WAY! SHOULD WE TRY TO STOP THEM?
WITH BB GUNS??

GO ON TO THE NEXT PAGE.

The animals are almost on top of you!

WILL YOU . . .

. . . use your weapons?
TURN TO PAGE 29.

. . . drop the BB guns and run?
TURN TO PAGE 79.

You agree with Rick. There are three of you. What can it hurt to talk to her?

"Where's the hiding place?" you ask as you walk over.

She gives you a wide smile. Wider than you've ever seen. Her teeth . . . they're green like old copper. And sharp. And she's got way too many!

"Right here in my well!" she cackles.

Her hands turn into claws and latch onto you, cutting through your coat and into your skin.

You struggle, but she drags you over the well's edge. Your fingers grasp the top of the well for a moment, but her weight pulls you down into the dark.

You hear your friends scream your name. The last thing you see is their frightened faces watching you fall.

THE END

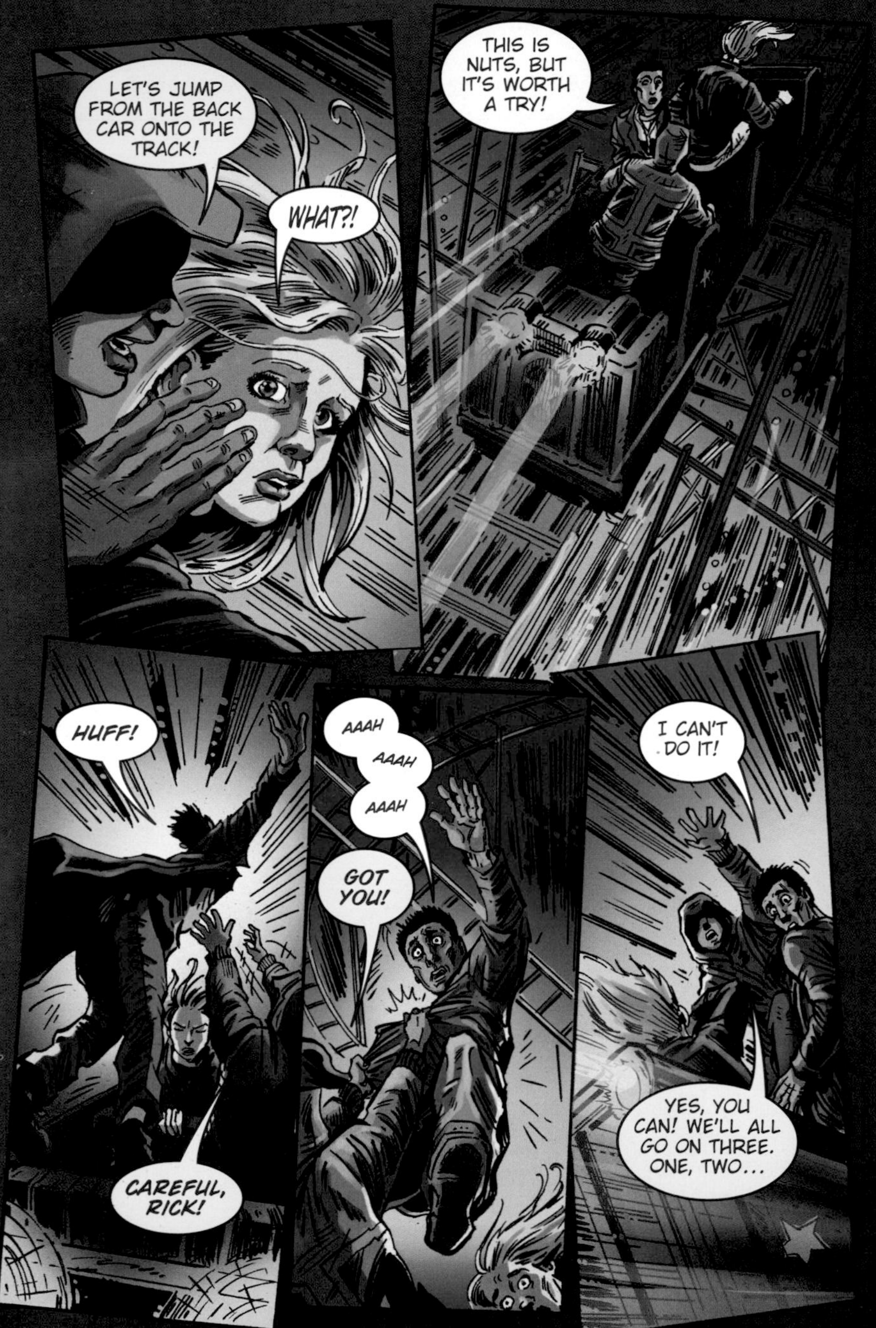
LET'S JUMP FROM THE BACK CAR ONTO THE TRACK!
WHAT?!
THIS IS NUTS, BUT IT'S WORTH A TRY!
HUFF!
CAREFUL, RICK!
AAAH
AAAH
AAAH
GOT YOU!
I CAN'T DO IT!
YES, YOU CAN! WE'LL ALL GO ON THREE. ONE, TWO...

GO ON TO PAGE 64.

You and your friends exchange helpless glances.

"We have to!" says Rick.

"Fine," you tell Setter. "We'll take you."

"Excellent," says the pooka. "You'll find the fence quite cool now."

Reaching out, you don't feel any heat.

"Now," says the pooka, "spread a semicircle of salt to protect us as we climb."

Sullenly, Rick and Laura do as it says.

"How are we going to carry something your size?" you ask.

"I'll be smaller," says Setter, turning into an eagle and perching on your pack.

Before long, you're over the fence and through the rowan trees. Setter leaps to the ground, a dog once more.

"Hey, wait! How did you make the fence hot? Isn't it made of steel?"

The pooka barks a laugh. "It is. And I didn't. It was just an illusion. All in your head!"

As the pooka disappears into the woods, it calls back, "You mortals are so gullible!"

THE END

WHICH TWISTED JOURNEYS®
WILL YOU TRY NEXT?

#01 CAPTURED BY PIRATES

#02 ESCAPE FROM PYRAMID X

#03 TERROR IN GHOST MANSION

#04 THE TREASURE OF MOUNT FATE

#05 NIGHTMARE ON ZOMBIE ISLAND

#06 THE TIME TRAVEL TRAP

#07 VAMPIRE HUNT

#08 ALIEN INCIDENT ON PLANET J

#09 AGENT MONGOOSE AND THE HYPNO-BEAM SCHEME

#10 THE GOBLIN KING

#11 SHIPWRECKED ON MAD ISLAND

#12 KUNG FU MASTERS

#13 SCHOOL OF EVIL

#14 ATTACK OF THE MUTANT METEORS

#15 AGENT MONGOOSE AND THE ATTACK OF THE GIANT INSECTS

#16 THE QUEST FOR DRAGON MOUNTAIN

#17 DETECTIVE FRANKENSTEIN

#18 HORROR IN SPACE

#19 THE FIFTH MUSKETEER

#20 PERIL AT SUMMERLAND PARK